Time May
Never Tell

A **Time Travel** Murder Mystery

WILL REID

WillReidBooks.com

Gratitude to all who read, chatted and kindly gave feedback. You know who you are…plus, of course, my 'Mrs Reid' who endlessly discussed every iota of the book in detail with me. Much Love.

ONE

DISCOVERY

"Run!" Phil was slow, and Steve knew it. "Keep up!" If either of them got caught, it would implicate the other.

They hurtled down the driveway of a large mansion house, with backpacks full of stolen loot. The humidity made their clothing grow heavier and clingier, as their burning lungs made it tough to go any further. A gunshot from behind gave them all the encouragement required, and their pace picked up.

Long, gnarly tree branches and curves in the driveway helped them avoid a clear shot by the gun wielding homeowner. They sped through the grand gated entrance, crossed the road, cleared the fence surrounding the woods, and vanished into the night.

A five-minute run through bushes and brambles, and dipping under branches, brought them to safety. Their hearts burst out of their chests as sweat stung their eyes. With rubbery legs barely holding them up, they caught a breather by a tree. The sweet scent of lavender and sound of chirping crickets provided a soothing contrast to the exhilaration of evading bullets during a burglary.

Steve took small steps with hands on hips as he repeatedly wiped away the sweat. "That was intense. My heart is still racing so fast."

Phil nodded in agreement, whilst making O's with his mouth to control his breathing. "Yeah, no kidding. We should be in better shape if we're going to do this."

Steve couldn't help himself. "I don't think our fitness is the problem. It's the adrenaline rush that's hard to stop once we start."

"I hear you. But we got lucky this time." Phil took a few more deep breaths. "We need to be more careful in future. We can't let our guard down like tonight."

Steve agreed, still blinking and wiping the sweat away. "What we need is a much better plan next time. Let's take a break for a while until things cool down."

Phil looked around, making sure no one was following. "That's a good idea. Let's regroup tomorrow."

The two thieves made their way through the wooded area and went their separate ways.

Steve was too hyper to sleep once he arrived home. Instead, he emptied his bounty onto the bedroom floor. Crouched down, he sifted through the items, estimating their worth; his attention drawn to two in particular.

An old pocket watch, which he found impossible to wind, seemed like a unique treasure. Steve played with it for a while, figuring out how to change the time, day, month, and year.

The second wasn't a watch. It was unlike anything he'd ever seen before, appearing to be of little monetary or practical value. A metallic exterior surrounding its cylindrical shape was both smooth and textured. Someone had originally polished the metal, but the scratches, nicks, and tarnished surface indicated its best days had passed. Several brass-looking knobs had to serve some purpose, but he could not fathom what that might be. However, when twisted, letters and numbers on its dials changed.

Steve intended to go to bed, but curiosity drew him back to tinker with them a little more. Both contraptions lay in his hands as he considered their worth, before twisting and turning the strange device's knobs until, for some unknown reason, the dials no longer turned. Nothing had come from any of his fiddling, so he gave up on it.

A closer inspection of the watch led him to believe it must be broken. "Piece of junk!" In frustration, he shook both contraptions, as if violence would somehow bring them to life. In a way, it did for the cylindrical device, as a sudden blinding light emanated from it ... and he vanished.

* * *

June 2023, Hometown

John lived in a quaint town, cradled amidst rolling hills, a stone's throw from the heart of nowhere. At least, that's how he described it.

His brief respite from the mundane nine-to-five routine each day was to peruse the community bulletin board at work.

One particular day, an eclectic collage of local announcements, advertisements, and forthcoming events kept him interested, as the peanut butter and jelly oozed from the sides of his sandwich. The board was a veritable smorgasbord of peculiarities and curiosities, unlike his lunch.

There was a flyer advertising a once in 50-year event at the school on Saturday; a notice for the monthly Culinary Club set for the upcoming Sunday; and an ad for the used car dealership, that claimed a "Once In A Lifetime" deal - every day.

One poster caught his eye: *Harding Estate Sale. This Weekend!*

The prospect of stumbling upon extraordinary and hidden treasures amidst a sea of unwanted cast-offs and trinkets beckoned. He imagined finding something that would submerge him deep into a world that mirrored the adventures he watched and read about. What such an item might be, he had no clue.

His imagination could not foresee life leading to anything other than the usual humdrum existence. So, the mere possibility of any sort of excitement was enough to spur him on. A headlong plunge into the bustling crowds of bargain-hunters, risking the very fabric of his sanity, would not deter him.

That radiant Saturday morning, the sun shone with such brilliance that it almost needed shades of its own. The fresh air carried scents of blooming flowers and next door's cut grass. John would usually have taken a deep breath and enjoyed it all. However, Friday night drinks still haunted him as he wretched, with a tongue rough as sandpaper and a head throbbing from too many rum and cokes. Only determination and deep concentration drove him without incident to the morning's outing.

On arrival, he joined the masses strolling down the hill. Everyone seemed intent on seeing inside the biggest house in town and picking up some bargains. Despite the heat and humidity, the atmosphere was electric, and he couldn't help getting caught up in the buzz of it all. At the entrance to the estate, he was in awe of the grand wrought-iron gates, adorned with intricate scrollwork and pillars on either side. These were by far the tallest gates John had ever seen.

The winding driveway, with towering trees that cast dappled shadows on the dusty path, was a maze for someone with a head that whirled like a tornado. There were a few stumbles, as he mistook a stone for a shadow and vice versa. A minute later, the imposing façade of the main house came into view. Ivy and climbing roses adorned red brick walls, and the windows gleamed in the sunlight. Intricately carved, the massive wooden front door seemed to tell its own story.

The soaring ceiling, accessorised with a single crystal chandelier, impressed as he entered the foyer. Down the hallway, rows upon rows of antique furniture, old books and assorted oddities awaited willing bargain-hunters. A few steps more, and he walked into a large ballroom, in which ornate candelabras and a spectacular, gilded mirror drew his gaze. Each had seen better days, but still held a modicum of splendour. He imagined that opulence must have once pervaded everything both inside and out. Today, however, long, threadbare, and faded velvet curtains told a story that he saw reflected throughout the house.

The bleary-eyed vision of his reflection in the polished marble floor encouraged him to have a sit down. He stumbled into a room filled with exotic plants and flowers where a seat awaited. With a deep intake of potent scents, he became a tad overwhelmed by 'men's-morning-sickness', an affliction he'd learnt went alongside male menopause, and being unable to find Tabasco in the fridge after someone else put it away. An appreciation of the flora's beauty, though, relaxed his mind and stomach, as the peaceful glow of sunlight streamed through coloured glass.

The more he saw, the more his amazement grew at the unbelievable wealth and luxury the Harding family had amassed. An abundance of barely used objects and a battered old G.I. Joe action figure, which stood out from all the grown-up stuff, sparked the recollection of what befell the family long ago.

John turned to the lady beside him. "Do you remember the tragedy that befell the Hardings years back?"

"Don't we all?" A scowl formed on her face. "It was a terrible affliction on the town's reputation when their nephew disappeared under such suspicious circumstances."

John couldn't help but feel a touch of melancholy, wondering whether this void in the Harding legacy contributed to the sale. He knew about Mr. Harding's passing a year prior, which he figured may have also influenced this mass clear out.

The occasional interesting item caught his eye. A picture frame stood out, not so much for its gaudy appearance, although it was over the top, but more for the colour photo it displayed. It looked photoshopped, as the scene appeared to be from the 1940s, but its clarity dispelled that possibility. It wasn't the frame or the image that drew his attention, though, it was the beauty of the woman walking towards the lens. He couldn't stifle his laughter, however, when he noticed that the man beside her was his doppelgänger.

"If only!" His wistful gaze focused on the couple.

Further along he discovered a dusty old box tucked away in a corner, probably untouched for many years.

"Ooh! Now that's the kind of thing I've been looking for." His heart raced as he lifted the lid, revealing a treasure trove of junk: broken clocks, rusty silverware, and old books.

A small, battered pocket watch at the bottom caught his attention amidst all the dross. It was no diamond in the rough, but more of a lump of coal in the mud. To John, however, it was a jewel. His sense of achievement was like finding a pair of socks that actually matched.

Old and dented, with a tarnished exterior, suggested someone had hidden it away for years. The face showed signs of cracks or scratches; he couldn't quite tell. While the hands looked to have stopped back when Big Ben was little. There was still an authenticity, though, that caught the eye. Most impressive for John was including the year in the date. That seemed unusual, and unusual was precisely what he was after.

Curious, he went to wind it by turning the crown wheel, but that only adjusted the time. When the crown pulled out and turned, that adjusted the date. He inspected it further, turning it over and over, but couldn't find a winding mechanism. However, an engraving on the back intrigued him. "Time May Tell". No markings indicated its origin or value, but something about its weight hinted at luxury despite the outward appearance.

John had his first find of the day, so pocketed the watch and moved deeper into the competing throngs of bargain-hunters.

His eyes darted back and forth, scanning for anything interesting. While sifting through a pile of knick-knacks on a rickety old table, he knocked into a teenage boy beside him, whose attention was on a blonde girl across the room. The shock of being knocked startled the boy, and he began a domino effect of item after item toppling over on the table. A small contraption on the edge teetered as it became the final domino. For a moment, it looked to be safe, but just breached the point of no return and tumbled towards the ground. John lashed out and grabbed it with the reflexes of a Major League catcher.

Once in hand, John took an interest in this newfound object, fascinated by how everything about it seemed odd, and scrutinised it in detail. Extensive use over many years had left it aged and worn, but some unknown, unique quality captured his imagination.

"I want that." The teenager made a grab for it. "I was about to get it when you hit me." He looked towards the blond girl, winked and mouthed, "Not really." as John turned away to protect his find.

"If I decide I don't want it, you can have it."

"Nah, grandpa. Give it to me."

John turned to shield the object from the boy and walked away to inquire about its price. He approached a teapot-shaped woman who clearly ran the whole show. She was buzzing around like a bee on a mission. It appeared as if she was everywhere all at once, rearranging items and barking orders at her helpers.

Mrs. Harding was strong-minded, with a powerful presence. She'd recently retired as a librarian after many years' loyal service. With her husband's passing, she was now alone on a vast estate with more useless objects and old forgotten relics than anyone could hope to find.

John cleared his throat. "Excuse me, ma'am. Could you tell me anything about this contraption?" He held up the strange device.

She paused for a moment and looked at him over the top of her glasses. "Hmm," she said, giving him a look like a confused flamingo. "It's some old thingamajig my husband left behind. I haven't the foggiest clue what it is or does." Then her eyes gleamed with mischief. "Maybe it's a fancy hat rack. Who knows?"

She took the device from John and turned it over in her hands. "It looks like some kind of machine, but beyond that, I couldn't tell you."

John nodded with disappointment at the old woman's lack of guidance.

She handed it back. "You can have it for five dollars."

"Can I try to figure it out and let you have the cash if I find it's something I want?"

"Listen son. Just show me the money. I'm sure you'll have better luck figuring it out than I did."

Grinning, he dug a five-dollar bill from his pocket. "I'll give it a shot."

"Here's ten dollars, lady." The teenager butted in and waved a crisp ten-dollar bill in her face.

"Looks like you have some competition." A smug grin formed on Mrs Harding's face. "I'll happily take a ten over a five."

Surprised by the competition, John countered with a confident air of superiority, "Twenty."

Mrs Harding laughed. "This is getting fun."

"OK, old man. We can keep going up and up in price, and make this lady even richer, or we can settle this like men."

"Like men?" John thought that was a great line. "What do you suggest?"

"Rock, paper, scissors. Best of three."

Unsure of his win loss ratio, John considered his options. "OK, but we need an impartial referee."

"That'll be me," chirped Mrs Harding. She got them both in position and counted, "One, two, three."

"Yes!" shouted the boy, as his rock beat John's scissors. "You're one away from being whitewashed, Willie."

John rolled his eyes and set up for round two.

"One, two, three."

The boy's hand showed paper but moved it to rock when he saw John's scissors.

"No cheating." Mrs Harding adjudicated. "One to one. Final round."

Both held their hand in place, ready to do battle.

"One, two, three."

At that moment, John felt a sharp kick to his ankle, but Mrs Harding was unaware of the skullduggery. He had meant to play scissors, but the shock made him open his hand.

"You win." Mrs Harding shook John's hand. "Twenty bucks."

"No coffee for the next week." John counted the cash and handed it over. "To be honest. All I wanted was to beat that dumb kid."

He retraced his steps down the driveway with comparative ease, his head having cleared. It was now the crowd noise emanating from the nearby school that pinged his curiosity, leading him towards the school gates.

A group of students, parents, and local dignitaries had gathered. There were at least three hundred people, and despite his nonchalant efforts to see into the crowd, the sheer numbers blocked his path. It was like trying to navigate rush hour traffic in a clown car. So, he gave it a miss, removed himself from the crush, and began the walk up to his car.

Halfway up the hill, the excitement behind him grew louder and louder until a sudden hush tweaked John's curiosity, causing him to turn and peer down into the schoolyard. An opened capsule was the centre of attention as everyone huddled around and pointed at the object beside it. This led to a strange murmuring as onlookers appeared shocked. He hesitated and strained to see what was so interesting, but keen to try out his new toys, drove home instead.

As he pulled into the driveway of his modest house, John noticed his neighbour, Alice. She loved gardening and always kept her property immaculate. He waved while getting out of the car, and she smiled back. John's soft spot for her ever since they were teens had influenced his relationships with women. As an adult, though, he'd never acted on this impulse. His imagination couldn't see beyond the first couple of dates they went on as kids; but that's another story.

"John, what have you been up to?" Alice stopped weeding her vegetable patch and came over for a chat.

"Not much. Just exploring the space-time continuum." John loved to wind her up with oddball comments.

"Exploring what?" She screwed her face into a picture of astonishment.

He winked and grinned. "You know, time travel stuff."

Alice rolled her eyes. "Thought you said Sci-Fi wasn't real."

"Well, that's true. It's more a bunch of bollocks than science." John turned to walk towards his house.

She shook her head. "Did you find anything interesting at that estate sale of yours? Anything I might want to borrow?"

John stopped and produced the strange device from a bag to show it off. "As a matter of fact, I did. I found this crazy-looking thingamajig."

Alice examined it with great interest from her side of the fence. "Hmm, looks like something from one of your movies."

"Exactly! That's what I'm hoping," he said with a cheeky smirk.

"Don't get too carried away with your futuristic adventures, John. You still have to mow your lawn." Alice encouraged all her neighbours to be as proud of their garden as she was of hers.

"You would have me mow every day. Give me a break."

"I would. The smell of newly mown grass is ten times better than any man's perfume."

"Our natural perfume, you mean?" He took a whiff of both armpits and grimaced, finding his own natural perfume to be more horrendous than he'd expected.

Alice returned to her weeds. "Grow up, John."

"I'm not into gardening like you." He turned towards his house once more. "Time travel must indupitably have more going for it than yard work, though."

"Tell that to the weeds," she said, digging out some dandelions.

John leant over. "I bet time travel has a lot more going for it than yard work," he said to the dandelions and crabgrass.

"See you tomorrow, Alice." He headed inside, eager to unlock the secrets of his newfound treasure.

Slouched on the couch, an uncomfortable bulge in his pocket caught him by surprise. "What the heck?" Then it dawned on him. "Whoops! I didn't pay for the watch." He retrieved it and peered at his tarnished reflection in its rough exterior. The watch oozed history and character. "I'd love to hear your stories," he told the inanimate object, the likes of which often seemed to listen to him better than people.

The strange contraption, however, had him perplexed. Nothing about it made any sense. He poked and prodded it like a mad scientist, trying to make heads or tails of the thing. Repeated attempts to get it to do something were unsuccessful. A long-lost buddy type of chat had no effect, either. It even got a slap, like he was waking it up from a bender (but without the bucket of ice water in the face).

After hours, he admitted defeat. "Well, I'll be damned," he muttered to himself. "I guess this thing is nothing but a piece of junk." With that, he threw it in the corner and retired to bed, considering what else twenty dollars could have bought.

On the precipice of drifting into sleepy-bye-bye-land, something seemed to nag at him from the corner of the room. Was it all in his mind, or was it the device? John couldn't ignore it.

He picked up the watch to find the time, forgetting it was a useless timekeeper, so grabbed the device as well, but lost his balance and fell backwards onto the couch. With a vigorous shake of the device, he shouted, "Let me sleep!" However, before he could turn back to his bed, a brilliant light shot from within the device, causing him to shield his eyes.

Tuesday 28th January 1986, 10.58am, Hometown

John unfurled his arms and took a peek. Why was he on a different couch? And why was it no longer nighttime?

"Hang on!" he said out loud. "This place looks familiar." His eyes opened fully as his brain struggled to recognise the surroundings.

A voice grew louder as someone walked up the hallway. "John? John, are you there?" John froze, recognising that voice.

"Tom?" John stood up. "Is that you?" He hadn't seen or spoken to

Tom in years, so why would he be contacting him now?

Around the corner walked a teenage boy with ripped jeans, a heavy jacket and a yellow woolly hat. "Who are you?" came the response.

John leaned forward to get a good look at the youngster. "You haven't changed a bit." His eyes almost bulged out of their sockets. "Wow! You look identical to forty years ago in High School!"

A diminutive figure in stature, but full of personality, Tom was a heady mix of talent and torture for those that knew him. "Is John here?"

"Indubitably, you must be Tom's son?" John's expression changed to a frown.

"Why would I have a son? I'm only sixteen." Tom inched towards a coffee table and grabbed at a copy of that week's US Weekly magazine to use as a weapon. "Who are you, old man? And why are you in John's house?"

"Hey! Don't damage that magazine, son. That has to be a collector's item. Could be worth a few bucks." But then John took a closer look around the room. "No Way! How did I get here?" He walked around, touching furniture, shelves, and even the floor. "This is my parents' house."

"Yeah, right! You're older than John's parents. You can't be his brother. He doesn't even have a brother."

"I'm John. You know, John. I think we were at school together." The nostalgia and memories flooded back.

"John is my best friend. Are you his Uncle?"

"Er, no. I'm John, from school." He shook his head. "What am I saying?" Confused by inconsistencies, he hoped it was a trick of the mind or the light. But as they stood staring at each other, it became impossible to deny. The boy in front of him could only be his friend from forty years ago.

He couldn't help himself and blurted out, "Dude, you must have discovered the fountain of youth!" Stifled laughter followed as he waited for Tom's reaction.

Tom took immediate offence, having often been mistaken for being younger than his friends. The single raised eyebrow and scowled face illustrated how unamused he was. However, as John laughed out loud, Tom's expression softened, and a sly smile slipped out.

"You're ridiculous. You know that?" Tom gave in and joined the laughter.

From nowhere, John had an epiphany which gave him goosebumps. The device and watch he'd now stashed in his pockets had something to do with the flash of light. What happened while he covered his eyes? The thought came to him that perhaps Tom was not only younger, but from a different time altogether. Had the light flash transported him to an entirely different place and time? His mind was going a million miles a minute considering that he'd either gone back in time, or totally nuts. Neither scenario appealed.

He had heard stories of time travel and read up on the subject. For John, however, it was right up there with the earth being flat or the crazy notion that crunchy peanut butter doesn't go well with banana. Such scepticism had always made prefect sense. Yet here he was, standing in what he now realised was his parents' old living room. That distinctive leather couch smell and his burn mark on the coffee table were unmistakable. The possibility that he was having a face-to-face conversation with a teenage friend he'd lost touch with long ago, only added to the surrealism.

All there was to do, he decided, was to play along and hope to calm his nerves. "What's today's date?"

"January 28th. Why?"

"And the year?" The pitch of John's voice rose.

"What? You gone crazy? 1986, of course!" Tom looked at John with what he called his psycho-face.

"Oh No! Indupitably, you've got to be kidding me!" John's eyes widened. "Has the space shuttle Challenger exploded yet?"

Tom stared back in total disbelief. "I came over hoping to watch the launch with John. Has it exploded? Before take-off? Did you find my stash of magic mushies?"

It was 11.15am, so John switched on the TV. Tom watched, disinterested at first. "What channel is this? Never seen this before."

"It's CNN, of course." John, filled with trepidation, sat down.

Copying John, Tom lowered himself onto the couch. "Never heard of it. I watch NBC."

John struggled to process his predicament. Events were unfolding so fast that his grasp on reality fluctuated between somewhat insane through to plain stupid. "Am I about to see this calamitous moment in history again?" Beads of sweat formed on his forehead.

They watched the countdown in cautious silence. Tom lay back on the couch while John sat bolt upright, his pulse racing as the shuttle left the pad and soared into the sky.

A few seconds later...

Tom's mind exploded. "What the? Where'd they go?" He rushed forward to inspect the screen, his heart pounding in his chest. "How did you know? How could you possibly know that would happen?" He collapsed back onto the couch.

"I'm unsure whether to freak out or be impressed by your superpowers, old man. What I do know is, I'm outta here!" Tom turned to run.

John grabbed him by the arm, looked right into his eyes and said, "Wait, give me five minutes to explain."

As they talked, Tom noticed something strange. John implied

knowledge of future events by mentioning them before they happened. He spoke about smartphones, self-driving cars and virtual reality as if they were everyday objects. These ideas sounded too fantastical to be possible within the next hundred years. Donald Trump, as President, though, blew his mind. He wanted to know, "Who was Vice President, The Terminator?"

Tom's face belied his confusion. "How can you be an adult today with not much hair, and what you do have is mostly grey, when yesterday you were a pimply-faced teenager with braces and a bad haircut?"

"What bad haircut?" Now John took offence. "My dad used to do a great job cutting my hair."

"Yeah! If you want to look like a Cabbage Patch Doll." Tom's honesty was sometimes troubling. The more they talked, the more Tom noticed how John made a popping noise with his lips when there was a pause in the conversation, something particular to his sixteen-year-old friend. "I'm still not convinced you are who you claim to be." He stood back and eyed John up and down. "Prove it," he said.

John had a quick think. "What's the first thing you bought when you stole your dad's wallet last month?"

"Cigarettes." Tom's eyes narrowed as he observed John's reaction.

"No, it wasn't. It was a birthday present for your dad. I've never forgotten how crazy that seemed."

"But how would you know that?" Tom's expression made John laugh again. "No one knows that."

"Not yet they don't. But a few days from now, I think it is, you'll boast about it," he said with a glint in his eye.

"And what number am I thinking of?" Tom wanted an immediate answer.

John snapped back. "One."

"Ok, I don't know how this is happening, but you're John!"

"Of course, I am. You always say you only think about number one." John's grin was so smug. "I do wonder which number one you mean when you say that, though. If you preferred number two, I would worry."

John's looks were pretty leathery in parts, but he had the same dumb sense of fun Tom knew.

"You have to be John. No other person in The Universe has your wacky way of thinking. You ain't grown up much, either. And I cannot believe that you still say indupitably. It's not even a proper word."

"Yes, it is."

"It is not! What does it mean, then?"

"Definitely or without a doubt." John's nostrils began to flare.

"No. That word is indubitably with a b, not a p. And maybe only three people in the world, and a cartoon character, use it."

"Are you sure? I've always said it like that, though."

"Yip! Some things never change." Tom's eyes widened as he turned, noticing how his friend had aged beyond what time should have allowed. "John, you look... you look so... different."

John grinned and gave a knowing nod. He raised his hand and pointed two fingers at his own temple before turning them around to signify the concept of time travel.

Tom's mouth fell open in disbelief. He pointed to John and then to himself, as if to ask, "Are you a time traveller?"

John nodded.

"Woah! And I always thought I was more wacked out than you!"

A sense of excitement grew as they considered what might lie ahead. It was especially cool that they were together in this zany time warp thingy.

This was a new level of adventure for Tom, who always knew

where to find fun. His parents gave him a free rein to live his life his way. He was at liberty to visit school when he chose, stay out all night or hitch Route 66. They weren't concerned. His dad's only advice had been, "Every day is like a piece of pie, and your life experiences are your pie. Go eat your pie, son." At first, Tom had been unsure whether his father was serious, joking, or high. When he looked up into his eyes, though, the one thing he was sure about, his dad wasn't joking.

Tom turned to his aged friend, and with a face filled with glee, announced, "Life's about to get a whole load more interesting."

For John, a twinge of fear and uncertainty tempered the excitement. This was uncharted territory, and, as far as he was aware, it was uncharted for the entire human race. He expected to find a way home, but for right now, he was not confident as to the outcome of this mystical experience.

He stared into Tom's seemingly ageless face. "This was the break from the mundane I've been searching for. Funny how I had to meet you again to rediscover how fun life can be."

John had stumbled upon a time machine by chance and was keen to share his discovery with Tom. He brought out the watch and tried to explain how he had travelled through time.

"Great!" Tom said. "But do you know how to use it?"

"Not really, no," John replied. "Well, maybe?"

John, being older and possibly more mature, took charge, making it clear that they had to be careful not to run into John's younger self. That could have dire consequences for both of them. He took responsibility for his young friend and wanted to protect him from unknown drawbacks time travel might cause. They agreed he would be the only one to time travel. Perhaps not so much agreed, as John dictated. Unaccustomed to limitations, Tom said he liked that John cared enough to say no.

At that moment, however, John's heart sank. His parents' car pulled up to the house. Without a word, Tom escaped through the back door, around the front, and down the road, evading detection.

John also needed to make a hasty escape. He was no spring chicken like Tom. Making a run for it wasn't on the cards.

Trapped, with all exits only leading to his detection, John froze.

TWO

TIME TRAVEL 101

The jiggling of keys snapped John out of his trance. He scarpered up the stairs in a frantic search for a hiding place. At the top, a childhood memory was right in front of him.

The front door opened and his parents' voices grew louder. He slipped into the hall closet and closed the door, hoping against hope that no one would find him. This closet was often an effective sanctuary as a child, but he'd never had to squeeze himself inside before. Rancid odours from someone's unwashed socks and a manky t-shirt made him wretch. When he hid before, his mother threatened that it wouldn't be worth living if she found him. He considered the consequences could be far worse if she found him now.

Footsteps grew ever closer. He held his breath and prayed they wouldn't add to the laundry pile. His predicament was about to take an unfortunate turn.

John's father stood outside the closet door and called out. "Just going to the bathroom, Darl." He took one step, and there was a loud pffft sound. A few seconds later, John experienced excruciating nausea and a near lack of consciousness, as he fought against inhaling the noxious fumes of his dad's fart. Breaking point was close as he heard the toilet seat go down. It had seemed like an eternity, but now he burst out of the closet, gasping and purple in the face.

He'd hoped to remain incognito, but the deep breaths and inadvertent stepping on the cat, who had come to say hello thinking this was the John she knew, made such a racket. The tree outside his bedroom window looked like a potential escape route, so he ran for it and slid out onto a branch. His heart pounded as he heard his father shouting, "What the hell are you doing out there?" He descended, not so much climbing down as falling down.

Convinced that the thud when he hit the ground would lead to his discovery, John, in an instant, regressed back to his childhood. Filled with fear, he envisaged having to explain himself to his parents. Memories of the consequences of being a naughty boy resurfaced, causing him to pee himself just a little. After regaining some composure, as much as you can when there's a wet patch on your trousers, he remembered he was a man in his fifties. Back on his feet, he ran as fast as when only forty years old.

Tom waited at the end of the street, and John caught him up, stopping for a breather. He'd escaped the house undetected, which brought a sense of relief, although tinged with sadness.

"To have spent even five minutes with my parents would have made my day. I haven't seen them since an accident twenty years ago." He turned, looking back as he welled up.

"What's wrong with you, dude?" Tom was not one to mince words. "Go knock on the door."

John needed little convincing. So, after settling his breathing, he returned to the house.

His mother came walking round from the back garden. "Can I help you?"

John's legs buckled a little as he struggled to speak. "I was walking by and something about our, I mean, your house looked so beautiful. I wanted to stop and tell you. Is that OK?"

John's father appeared at the front door. "Everything alright?"

"Yes, Dear. This nice man wanted to tell us how much he appreciated our house. And pull up your zip. You're flying low."

With head down trying to find the zip handle, his dad said, "Do you want to buy it?" He always looked for ways to make money.

"No, sir." John paused, looking up at his mother, and across to his father, his head still tilted back, and resisting the urge to pop his lips nervously. "In fact, I wouldn't be surprised if your home reflects your family."

"Well, thank you." His mother was now standing beside her husband. "What a lovely thing to say. We are house-proud, as well as being very proud of our son, John. He's a little guy, but he's our little guy and we love him." And eyeing John from top to bottom, added, "Why, he's around your height. Funny that."

John paused for a moment, not moving an inch before breaking the awkward silence. "In case this were ever to happen, say on his seventeenth birthday, don't be too hard on … John, was it? He might smoke too much weed and drink too much of the old moonshine, resulting in you having to throw out your prized rug in the living room. That may sound random. But kids, eh? Gotta love 'em, right? Anyway, it was so nice to meet you."

His mother leant towards him and touched his arm. "Are you ok? You sound like you've smoked a bit too much weed recently. By the way, you didn't see anyone run out of here a few minutes ago, did you? I think we had a prowler."

"No. I didn't. Sorry." John smiled, paused once more and turned to rejoin Tom, who had observed the whole thing. John walked straight past him. "Let's go. I need to get outta here."

But Tom wasn't listening. Out of the corner of his eye, he'd noticed something and became transfixed by a passing bus. To his dismay, the distinctive figure of a pimply-faced teenager with braces and a 'not so bad' haircut sat with his arm wrapped around his girlfriend, Alice.

Tom turned towards John, pointing at the bus. "Who is that?"

John was still walking. "Who is what?"

"Why are you on that bus with Alice?" Tom stood motionless; disbelief etched on his face.

"I'm not. I'm here with you. Look." John exaggeratedly pointed a finger at himself.

Tom's pointing became more animated as he turned towards John. "Yes, you are! There is you and there is Alice. And you're on the bus, together. See?"

"Oh! True." John blushed. "I remember that. Not sure how to put this, my friend, but she won't be your girlfriend much longer."

"Stop telling me about the future! This is the present! She is still my girlfriend!" Snot and spit flew as Tom hurled his fury at John.

John wiped his face and looked at the ground, the hint of a blush appearing. "Yeah, we went on a date. I remember because it was only once I arrived home that I heard about the Shuttle. After such a great day, I was devastated."

Tom calmed down and blew his nose. "OK. I don't hold you responsible, old man, but I am gonna smash that guy when I next see him!"

"Great. You do that. No permanent scars, though. OK?" John's encounter with his parents still filled his thoughts. "I wanna get moving." He led Tom, who was scanning each parked car, down the quiet urban street.

"Pick a car, dude!" Tom slid his hand across the hood of a 1977 Cadillac.

"That one. If I had the money, that would be mine." John pointed to a sleek, black car.

"Nah, too flashy. We need something inconspicuous."

John stopped. "Inconspicuous for what?"

Tom continued walking. "What do you think?" A few cars later, he spotted an old, beat-up sedan.

"Perfect," Tom whispered with a sly grin.

A set of wire cutters was all he needed to crouch next to the driver's side and get to work; his fingers moving with purpose.

John wandered over and watched in amazement, hoping to learn a new skill. "Are you for real? Now I understand how you could afford both an Amiga 1000 and Apple II computer. That Apple could make you rich one day. Oh sorry. I'm telling your fortune again."

Tom wasn't listening, as with expert hands he stripped and twisted wires. After a few tense moments, the car roared to life. He flashed a cocky grin and slid into the driver's seat.

"Nah!" John wasn't ready to put his life in the hands of a sixteen-year-old thief. "Move over, boy!" and pushed him aside. Tom didn't argue, climbing into the passenger side.

"Where are we going?" The roads had changed little, but John needed Tom to lead them to a safe haven.

"Drive! I'll navigate. My parents own a cabin a few hours away."

Within minutes, they were out of town and on the open road. Neither was in the mood for a chat with their minds miles away.

The sun set over the countryside, painting the sky in hues of orange, pink and purple. Ahead, the road snaked through lush green fields and rolling hills which seemed to stretch on endlessly. In the distance, silhouetted trees against the horizon created a sight of serene beauty. A cool breeze blew in, carrying with it a heady mix of wildflowers and the whiff of manure. The car's hum broke the peaceful ambience as they bounced along the rugged terrain. Tom didn't seem to mind (he was probably pondering what to do about Alice).

By the time they approached the cabin, the sun had set, and the trees were much taller, forming a darkened canopy. With headlights on beam, the car slowed to a crawl. Off the main road, they turned onto a dirt path which wound through towering poplars.

The cabin came into view, its wooden exterior blending with the natural surroundings. It was a cozy, rustic abode, and the desire for a warm fire flickering in the hearth, with the aroma of wood-smoke, was all the encouragement needed to get inside.

After the fire was lit, Tom laid back on the large plaid sofa. "The thing I love the most about this place is the smokiness of burning oak."

John chose one of the mismatched chairs and put his feet up on a rickety old table. "I love how this place gets you back to basics. It's a real treat for me to experience the great outdoors. Natural beauty surrounds Hometown, but I never go anywhere. Can't afford to with my mortgage."

The kitchen was small but stocked well, with pots and pans hanging from hooks above the stove, and a vintage beige refrigerator against one wall. Tom soon got stuck in and prepared a simple dinner, while John made his way up a narrow staircase to a small, sparse loft with a single bed and a small dresser. He didn't off load his shoes yet, knowing that his feet needed a wash to save Tom's nostrils. The bathroom was an outhouse, so John trounced outside, washed his feet, and got ready for dinner. Tom's culinary creation belied his years as, out of necessity, he'd taught himself to cook aged ten.

The reacquainted friends sat with only the dim light of the fire and a lantern. It was about time they learned how the devices functioned as a time machine. Tom believed setting the knobs and dials must have some meaning. They needed to understand the simplicity of its design.

Whilst at the sale, John had set the watch to 1986, so that must set the target time. Through trial and error, they discovered which knob did what and which dial took them where. John had disappeared three times, only to reappear one minute later; having been to the other side of the room five minutes earlier and the middle of the waist-high lake outside an hour ago. (That idea came from Tom, and didn't amuse John). The ultimate trip, though, was to the same location, one hundred and fifty million years in the past. When John reappeared, his clothes were smouldering. The whites of his eyes peered out in stark contrast to the black mud covering his face, and he had literally crapped himself. The sheer terror in his eyes was so acute and the smell so foul, that Tom didn't have the gumption to ask what happened. John had to clean himself up, and it was an hour before he stopped repeating, "Oh, crap!"

It was as if they had stepped into a crazy science professor's lab, where anything was possible, and nothing was unexpected. The two-way banter tapered off as they considered the implications of their newfound power.

Tom broke the silence. "What if we screw up big time? No one knows what happens when you screw up time and space. We could get in a whole heap of trouble. What do you think the sentence is for rewriting history?"

"Who's going to know? The Time Police? We need to do this properly, though, not like a couple of crackpot school kids. Let's set some ground rules. Maybe we shouldn't visit significant historical events, like World Wars or Dallas, in November 1963. And I think we will stay away from Paris in 1789."

"No going to Woodstock then?" Tom raised an eyebrow. "Yeah,

could create a butterfly effect. One slight change and the whole of human history goes nuts. Without careful planning, we might change someone like Neil Armstrong's life. Your President Trump could have become the first man on the moon instead."

John raised his eyebrows. "That's not such a bad idea. But I don't believe in butterfly effects. I thought time travel was impossible until a few hours ago. I've researched, and after reading blogs, watching YouTube, and even reading books around the subject, it seemed too fantastical to be true."

Tom looked confused. "What are blogs? Do you mean bogs? Do people write on bogs in 2023? That's some weird shit, man! And what's YouTube? A fancy TV channel? Is this twenty-first century old man crazy talk normal? Do I have this to look forward to?"

"No, listen." John wanted Tom to focus and laid out a couple of time travel theories he found interesting and considered plausible.

(Note to you, the reader: If you aren't interested in temporal theories, skip the next couple of paragraphs. Yes, the author is not meant to speak, but, hey, I don't want you snoring.)

"One is called the 'Novikov Self-consistency Principle', which says we cannot change historical events. The principle says that no matter what happens or how many times someone tries to change an event, the present and future are predetermined. The past will remain unchanged.

"Ooh sounds fancy." Tom showed no interest in that theory. "Anything less heavy duty?"

"There is a counter theory called the 'Many-worlds interpretation of quantum mechanics' which suggests that time travel could create alternate timelines, where time travel brings about different results."

Tom folded his arms and nodded. "Yeah, cool. I'll go with that."

John was unsure, so wanted to figure out how time travel worked.

"Who knows, right? I guess we'll find out as we go along. Let's tread carefully to avoid screw ups. We can get busy livin' or get busy dyin'."

"Huh? That's your crazy-old-man-talk again! Where does your weird way with words come from? Is it genetic?"

"It's from a movie. I could tell you the name, but you'd never remember it. You'll understand how we oldies think when you've lost your adenoids and you're praying to no longer feel those haemorrhoids." John's face mimicked his last bout of the painful ailment.

Tom shook his head. "Who is the grown up here?"

"I'll tell you what, though. It'd be fun to change some things."

"Oh yeah, like what?" Tom waited. "Come on, oh wise one. Expound those words of wisdom."

After a quick think, John had an idea. "The FIFA World Cup is later this year. Maradona from Argentina cheats and scores an important goal with his hand. I could shake his hand before the game, pretending I'm a fan, and squeeze it real hard, as in real hard! Should help deter him from banging the ball in with his fist. I could change sporting history."

John's response disappointed Tom, who proposed a more realistic idea. "How about you go back and stop yourself from stealing my girlfriend?"

To save his bacon, John retorted, "You know I can't meet myself and interchange space and time with my own flesh and blood. That could create a paradox, melting time itself! I don't want that on my conscience." Tom accepted that explanation, which was a relief for John, as he had no idea what he was talking about.

Tom had his thinking-cap on. "We can't just decide how we want time travel to work and go blasting around, causing havoc because we're wrong."

"True. We need to find out for ourselves." John paced the room. "How can we do that?"

Tom knew what to do. "You need to change something in the past. Let's see if it has a knock-on effect into the future."

"When I return, though, it had better not prevent you from being here. And it won't be a change for you. So, you'll need to take my word for it. Could this get any more complicated?"

"Yeah, makes sense. What do you want to change?" Both paced the room until Tom said, "A cousin of mine in Seattle is such a big mouth. He makes tons of money putting some computer stuff on IBM's computers. When we visit Seattle, he never pays for dinner, or even an ice cream. How about stuffing up his deal with IBM?"

"Are you sure?" Unconvinced, John continued, "It'll be a long shot, but I'll give it a go. We've nothing to lose." He got all the details from Tom, formulated a sketchy plan, and dressed in some of Tom's father's clothes. "I'm ready!"

Wednesday 20th August 1980, 9.30am, Boca Raton, Florida

With an uneasy feeling, like falling into an ocean without a life vest, John appeared outside IBM's offices. His aim was to find Tom's cousin and discredit him with IBM execs before negotiations began that would make him astronomically wealthy. John knew nothing about computers, but knew of Tom's world famous cousin back home in 2023. An early 1980s photo showed how much he'd changed .

Fifteen minutes passed, and someone who looked a lot like the photo came towards him. It was time to make his move.

With a lukewarm cup of coffee in hand, John, accidentally on purpose, walked into the guy, spilling it all over his shirt.

"You ruined my shirt! What made you … arrgh … can't you look where you're going?"

"Oh no! That looks terrible!" John resisted dabbing the guy's chest to clean up the mess. "I hope you didn't have anywhere important you needed to be."

"Only the most important pitch of my life!" His eyes darted in all directions.

"Listen, let me buy you a new shirt at Burdines. It won't take long. Town Center Mall is close by."

A quick look at his watch and the agitated businessman agreed. "You had better make this fast, mister."

After purchasing the shirt, John handed his victim a cold drink. "Take a minute to calm your nerves."

With the reluctance of a labrador going outside on a rainy day, the gullible geek gulped down a whole can of pineapple juice. Five minutes later, Tim Paterson was sleeping like a baby, propped up by a lingerie mannequin in Sears.

To nail the mission, John returned to IBM, to screw up any chance Seattle Computer Products would have of ever getting their foot in IBM's door again.

As the elevator doors were about to close and take him up to IBM's offices, an arm with a briefcase shot inside and the doors opened once more. A bespectacled young man entered and smiled somewhat bashfully, but with a confidence that gave John an idea.

He pushed his skewed glasses back onto his face, as they'd slipped in his rush to catch the elevator. "Fifteen, please."

"What's your name, son?"

"My name's Bill, sir."

"Do you know anything about computers?"

Bill began to blink rapidly, as though annoyed. "Yes, I do."

"Perfect!"

John summarised the Seattle Computer Products and IBM story for

Bill, attempting to convince him to grasp the opportunity of a lifetime.

The doors opened on the fifteenth floor, but Bill stayed in place and continued to the twenty-first. He stepped out of that elevator, walked straight up to the receptionist, and introduced himself. "Hi, I'm Bill Gates from Microsoft. Philip Estridge's 11am hasn't shown, has he?"

"No, Mr Gates, not yet." The receptionist took a breath.

"Allow me to provide what he was hoping for from that meeting." Bill's charm shone through. "Can I please have fifteen minutes? Believe me, I'll make it worth his while."

John watched, impressed by his choice, before riding the elevator alone, towards the ground floor, ensuring he wouldn't be inside once the doors opened.

Tuesday 28th January 1986, 9.30pm, Tom's Cabin

"I'm back!" John's anticipation was electric at having potentially fulfilled Tom's wishes. Now was the moment they'd discover how much, if at all, the world had changed.

"Cool. That was quick." Tom sat eating an ice cream.

Straight to the point, John asked, "How's your cousin, Tim?"

"How do you know Tim?" Tom looked at John through squinted eyes. "What's this to do with your plan?"

"Does he have some big contract with IBM to sell some computer software?" John's fingers wrapped on the table, waiting for an answer.

"Who? Tim? I don't think so." Tom seemed unsure what John was leading towards. "You're not getting him confused with Bill Gates, are you?"

"Ha! Ha!" John grabbed hold of Tom and swung him around the room. "I did it! We did it! We changed history! I can't believe it!" John jumped over tables, ran up and down stairs before continuing the celebratory antics outside.

Tom let John swing him, looking at him like he'd flipped.

John stopped the swinging and grabbed Tom by the shoulders. "I went to change history, right?"

Tom nodded. "Yeah."

"And you knew you'd be unaware of whether I did or not. True?"

Tom's eyes narrowed and his head tilted a touch. "Yeah."

John came to his point. "Before I left, your cousin Tim had a contract with IBM. I changed history and Bill Gates got that contract."

"You did what?" Tom came to life as the reality hit him. "You stopped my family from becoming super rich? Are you nuts?"

"No, but you were. It was your idea." John burst into uncontrollable laughter, as Tom appeared in two minds why he would even think of such a thing. He walked in one direction and then the other, all the while muttering to himself.

John ended up on the floor in pain. "I have not laughed like that since Alice got her nightgown caught on a branch in her garden, lost her balance, fell over and the gown came off."

"Alice? My girlfriend, Alice?" Tom approached John and stood over him. "Do you still know her?"

"Of course. She's my neighbour. Known her all my life." John was never great at empathising with someone else's matters of the heart. He hadn't considered the impact this news would have on his young friend.

"Is she your girlfriend? Or do you just hookup from time to time? When did you last hookup with her?" Tom's questions came thick and fast.

John wished he'd kept his mouth shut about Alice. "None of your business, but the answer to all your questions is no. Change the subject time."

Tom wanted details. "Was she naked when her gown came off?"

John shook his head. "No. That wouldn't have been half as funny as seeing her wearing Bananas In Pyjamas PJs, accessorised with cowboy boots. I nearly wet myself."

Tom went to bed. His mental image of John's story failed to have the same effect on him as it had on John.

"Is that it? Are you going to bed now? We now know that Novikov was wrong, and the other guys had it right all along. Time travel does change the future!" John's mind raced as he considered this to be a monumental discovery in human history.

Tom's reaction to the breaking news was less than enthusiastic. "OK. Fine. I'll accept that we found the truth. Fantastic! But while you're gallivanting through time, how will I know where you are?"

John had to think about that. "Hmm, good point." There were a few things to organise, and he knew he wasn't able to rush off like some mad scientist. "We need to agree when and where to meet."

They decided the next jump should be after a good night's sleep. John was to appear in a clearing near the cabin at 10am, six months from tomorrow. Tom would meet him there.

Next morning, the sun rose over the forest and John took in the view from the window overlooking the lake. Despite his excitement, there was unease, knowing he was about to step into an unknown labyrinth that may not welcome him.

Before leaving, John turned to Tom with deep sincerity. "I was thinking last night. There is something I want you to know." Tom backed off as John sounded way too intimate. "I remembered that the Kentucky Derby winner this year wins at odds of 17-1. Put everything you have on Ferdinand to win. May 3rd, in case you don't know."

"Phew!" Tom's inner voice inadvertently blurted out. "Thought you were going to kiss me!" After calming down, he wanted to be sure Ferdinand was a sure thing.

John's look of confidence brought a smile to Tom's face. "Alright!"

"OK, see you in six months." John set the watch and dials, took a gulp of fresh air, shook the gadget, and vanished.

* * *

Tom was alone in the clearing. He feared John would never return, or that the vast realms of time would swallow him whole. As the time ticked by, Tom made a promise to himself that he would be ready and waiting for John's return.

A minute later, Tom was at the clearing's edge as John reappeared .

"Ha! Did I do it?" John arrived at the spot where he'd disappeared. "Did you miss me?"

Tom's look of bewilderment made John laugh so hard that he fell over. "Why are you back already?"

As he regained his feet, both the watch and gadget fell into the dew-filled long grass. "I wanted to see the surprise on your face. It was priceless!" After picking up the powerful time travelling gadgets, the time had come to leave, as agreed. "OK, six months this time."

Tuesday 29th July 1986, 9.55am, The Clearing By Tom's Cabin

Tom fulfilled his promise to himself. He was in place and on time, as he thought John might need help.

Ten minutes later, John appeared.

"What happened to you, dude?" Tom's face was a picture of confusion. "You didn't look like that when you left six months ago."

He didn't know whether to be concerned or laugh, but the questions came think and fast. "Are you OK? Why are you covered in blood? And what's with the old-fashioned gear? Where have you been? When have you been?"

* * *

THREE

AN UNEXPECTED JOURNEY

Saturday 3rd May 1941, 12.05pm, Liverpool, England

A shudder shot down John's spine as he realised, "Whoops! This isn't the field."

Barrage balloons flew high over buildings, while men and women in military uniforms scurried by on foot or drove old cars. Billboards plastered everywhere advertised Camel cigarettes or encouraged everyone to "Keep Calm". Non-military types wore uncomfortable looking clothes and some of the architecture was like nothing he'd ever seen before.

"What the hell is this?" he thought. "Holy Crap! You are kidding me!" Reality hit him hard between the eyes. "Shit! This looks like World War Two!"

"No kidding!" responded a man who was standing on the corner of a cobble-stoned alley, watching John appear from nowhere. "Wake up and smell the porridge, mate!" And off he walked, disinterested at the potential apparition.

John's anguish at not having arrived at the lake wasn't his most pressing concern. "I need to get home," he said under his breath.

In disbelief, he stared at the devices in his hands. "This is not how I set you! Your settings must have changed when you fell in the grass." John had read about the stability of closed time-like curves influencing the detours of time travel. Those curves had turned out to be less closed and more like his Aunt Hilda's backside, unpredictable.

He tried to turn the gadget's dials and watch's hands, but they were stuck firm.

"Damn! They're broken!" His eyes bulged out of his skull, as he considered the implications. "Life at fifty wasn't supposed to be like this. I'm left with no friends, no family, nowhere to live and I'm minus thirty years old. This is crazy! I always mess things up and should never have played with this time travel stuff."He guessed that moisture from the dew had got into the mechanisms, causing them to jam, and it would only need a short while for them to dry out and become unstuck.

A personal interest in World War Two history from a young age, and having supported his local Veterans Association, meant the predicament very much appealed, as long as it was only temporary. So, quick to immerse himself in his fascinating new surroundings, he forgot about time travel for a while and dove into the whole experience.

Wherever this was, blending in and avoiding attention seemed like a good idea. The genuine risk of changing something at such a pivotal juncture in history garnered his thoughts to be alert to his surroundings. The street sign nearby read James Street, but James Street where? People walking by spoke a type of English, but he could barely understand their strong accent. Despite listening closely and hoping to get a clue, he remained lost, although he thought there was a hint of Irish.

In his disoriented state, he accidentally knocked into a passer-by. After apologising, he inquired as to the name of the town.

"You're in Liverpool, mate," came the response.

"Liverpool! In England? But that's on the other side of the ocean."

"Well, we ain't in Germany, are we? And we never will be!" The man walked away, less than impressed by John's strange question, as the whirring of sirens filled the air.

John's heart pounded, a sudden rush of adrenaline urging him to get off the street and seek cover. Instead he froze, unsure for a moment what his next move should be, but deciding to follow everyone else.

No one rushed, which seemed brave, that so many could be courteous and kind, knowing that at any moment, bombs could rain down on them. The sound of explosions came closer, though, and German aircraft were now overhead. A genuine sense of urgency became obvious and those in the open began to run.

With the naivety of a newcomer to air-raid shelters, John entered with no clue what he might find. The mustiness met his senses, which, although unpleasant, wasn't terrible. The sea of humanity, women and children huddled stoically beside the elderly, brought a lump to his throat. He descended into the dimly lit bunker to join them on rough wooden benches. Some sat, their eyes fixed on the ground. Others chatted away, keeping their minds off the dangers above. Despite the chatter, he sensed an atmosphere of resigned apprehension.

Headed for a free spot towards the back, he tripped and fell between a young woman and the wall.

"Oh, I am so very sorry!" His hands fumbled to reorganise the mess he'd created on her lap.

"Leave it! Leave it!" She pushed him away.

With great embarrassment, he squeezed onto the bench beside her, only to find that it dug into his spine.

His temporary acquaintances had likely been through so much already that he wondered at the stories of horror they could tell. There was no chance he was going to ask, though. "How would that have appeared?" he thought, as his eyelids drooped. "I'm from the future. What's it like living with the threat of bombs killing you and your entire family at any moment? I'm asking so I can tell my friends when I get out of this hell hole." In a dreamlike state of semiconsciousness, the insensitive scenario ended with a large woman slapping him across the face, a slap which woke him from the dream with a start.

Fearful the dream may have been real, he knelt and chatted with those on their own, and provided first aid for a child with a bumped knee. Relief washed over him when a lady offered him a scone, which he took as a sign of acceptance.

Everyone was in the same boat, and a keen sense of camaraderie grew, drawing them together. Children beginning to laugh and play, while the low hum of more elderly inhabitants' conversations brought some normality.

John's fashion sense stood out, though. Twenty-first century American attire defied the norms of 1940s England. Most other shelter residents seemed unfazed by his uniqueness. The vibrant colours and unusual patterns of his clothing caught the eye, while the fabric's rustling added some interest for a few bored individuals. A young boy approached him. "Hey Mister, what's with the weird clothes? Are you from Blackpool or something? You look like the illuminations."

John found the youngster's directness refreshing and funny. "Yeah, something like that. Let's focus on staying safe for now, okay?" The boy nodded, and they got chatting, for as long as the little guy could stay still.

With a mop-top of short red hair tucked under a small cap and freckled round face, the friendly boy named Joe gave John someone to befriend. He ran around, benefitting from interactions with a multitude of people, both young and old. Rationing meant he wore a jacket and trousers that were too long for him, which was fine as his mother probably thought he'd grow into them. John glimpsed her half trying to rein in the restless schoolboy while offering comforting words to those around. With drooped posture and tired eyes, she looked frazzled, but despite fatigue, summoned a tender smile for her boy. Her long locks of red hair cascaded down to her shoulders, adding a noticeable vibrancy that twinged a sense of familiarity in John.

"Do I know her?" he asked himself, approaching her with a fair amount of apprehension.

"This may sound strange, but you look fa…" Like a custard pie to the face, the realisation hit him full on. For several seconds, saying nothing, he stood with eyes wide open, mouth wide open and looking gormless. This was the woman in the photo at the Harding estate sale.

An awkward pause broke when she responded, "Sorry, I missed that. Were you talking to me?"

"Oh, sorry! I'm John. It seems that you're carrying the weight of everyone's expectations. Can I help?"

"I'm Joyce." Her brow, furrowed with worry, reflected her desire to help everyone. "I am well versed in getting through these air raids. My estranged husband is a warden. We recently experienced a bitter separation." She paused before berating herself. "Why did I tell you that?" She wrapped herself in her overcoat like a warm, comforting embrace.

The air raid continued for several hours, which gave John the opportunity to assist the most beautiful women he'd ever seen in a photo and later met eighty years earlier. He considered this chance meeting to be a profound coincidence designed by fate.

When the all-clear sounded, and everyone emerged from the

shelter, John offered to help mother and son navigate the debris of the bombed-out streets.

"That would be great, John. You are a love, helping me. It made the time go so much faster."

"I'm very pleased to have met you both."

"How far from here are you, John?"

"To be honest, too far." He wasn't sure how to answer. "In fact, I'm not meant to be here."

"That's a strange thing to say. I know you're American, but do you mean you're lost? Do you have a place to stay?"

"Well, er, no. I guess not." John looked away, embarrassed at appearing needy amidst those caught up in war.

Whilst in the shelter, the explosions had frightened even the hardiest resident. The thirty-minute walk to Joyce's passed through the devastating effects of war. Fires burned and they walked by dilapidated streets, affirming their fears.

Once they arrived, it seemed inappropriate to invite a strange man inside, so lively conversation continued on the doorstep while Joe played indoors. For more than an hour, a gentle drizzle dampened their clothes but not the warmth of each other's company.

The time came for John to bid farewell. With a nod, he turned to cross the street, at which his gaze met the intense stare of a young man in an alley, stopping him in his tracks. Unsure why he'd stopped, John peered through the soft dim lighting and edged towards the figure.

From twenty metres, the strange figure of a man seemed familiar. John drew closer and in a flash realised this looked like Brian Harding, the nephew who had disappeared from Hometown in 1986. His heart raced as he tried to make sense of this apparition. Brian looked somewhat older and rougher, with a beard and unkempt hair. The haunted eyes and face were unmistakable, though, just like he remembered from newspaper photos.

He approached with caution. "Brian? Is that you?"

The dishevelled man didn't respond, but now stared past John, his attention focussed on Joyce's home. Another chill ran down John's spine. He knew something unfathomable was happening. But as he drew closer, the man took off running, disappearing down the alley.

The encounter left John stunned. "What happened? This time travel malarkey is getting spooky. I'm pretty sure that was Brian."

Joyce emerged from a neighbouring house. "John, my neighbour Josey says you can stay at hers tonight. Does that work for you?"

John's scouse accent wasn't great but he wanted to try it out. "That'd be brilliant, like."

"Come on, then." Joyce beckoned him back.

An elderly woman welcomed him at her front door with a smile. "Stick to American. It's a lot sexier than that babble you attempted."

Joyce giggled. "I've never heard her say that to anyone before," and gave John a wink. "I'll be next door. If Josey doesn't keep you occupied, you're welcome to come for dinner."

John followed Josey to a small yet tidy room, with a bed and thick blanket. A lamp on the bedside table cast a soft glow across the room. He thanked her and before she could respond, zipped across to Joyce's for dinner.

They had just met, but the conversation continued to flow in a relaxed atmosphere, and all three enjoyed what John described as the perfect evening.

Joe showed off his St. Christopher with great pride. "Mum gave me this because one day I'm gonna travel far away. Aren't I Mum?"

"You certainly will, and St Christopher will protect you throughout the entire journey." She smiled, pulling him into her bosom.

John retired for the night, ensuring he'd firmly shut the bedroom door. He barely slept, tossing and turning on the thin mattress, hoping not to hear footsteps or the creaking of his bedroom door.

Morning came and John was so drained that he wondered why he'd bothered going to bed. The familiarity of chirping birds seemed to be in stark contrast to his surreal situation. To be living inside World War Two England, while bombs were falling, was so crazy he slapped himself twice to see if he'd wake up from a dream.

He didn't.

Joyce suggested checking out the ruins from the previous day. The trio made their way with sombre hearts through desolate streets. In typical Liverpudlian friendly fashion, a stranger commented how John's futuristic looking clothing wouldn't protect him from the wind and offered him a long overcoat.

The acrid smell of smoke and ash clouded the air as they passed houses on The Strand, approaching the corner with James Street. The ruined buildings were strewn with destroyed possessions. Joyce and Joe remained silent, their faces grim as they surveyed such horror.

John's sadness deepened as traces of fear and despair showed on Joyce's face. So, he welcomed what seemed like a desire for comfort, as she put her arm in his and snuggled in. Across the road, a man in a cap passed a demolished house where an air-raid warden stood atop the rubble, pools of smoke rising from the ruins around him.

Joe, walking with hands in his pockets, turned to see a police photographer capture the scene of destruction. Intrigued at being in the picture, he asked, "Hey mister. Can I get a copy of your photo?"

But the photographer wasn't interested. "Sorry son. Official police business only."

They continued to Joyce's brother's house, which was Joyce's usual Sunday afternoon jaunt. Joe had a grand old time with his cousins, while Joyce and John mingled with the locals. And what a bunch they were. Scousers, being full of wit and wisdom, taught John linguistically challenging phrases. It was like a comedy routine that put him in stitches of laughter, enjoying himself more than he had in ages.

Dinner ended, and they meandered home through the damp, cold streets of Liverpool. John was relieved to retreat to his room after a draining and emotional but enjoyable day. He hoped to sleep through the night and was soon snoring.

The sound of a scream shot him out of his slumber, unsure of what he'd heard, so lay awake, listening intently. A short time later, the loud thud of a door slamming came from Joyce's house.

John's room was dark; the sun had set and the birds no longer chirped. Groggy and disoriented, concern for Joyce compelled him to investigate the commotion. He rubbed his eyes, stretched his arms, and yawned before doing the necessaries in the bathroom. The coat, which he'd forgotten to return, went on, as Liverpool seemed cold most of the time, and he proceeded to Joyce's, thinking everything was probably alright.

The past few days seemed like some crazy dream to John. What happened next turned it into a nightmare.

He approached the front door, which, being open, made him cautious about entering. An eerie silence brought a deep unease.

"Joyce," he called out.

No response.

From the backyard, muffled footsteps echoed, their hurried rhythm hinting at more than one person fleeing through the gate.

With a pounding heart, John continued to take hesitant steps, consumed by an overwhelming dread. The emptiness of the living room and the mess in the dining room only solidified his fears, leaving little doubt there'd been a violent struggle. Determined, he pressed on into the kitchen.

There, sprawled face down on the floor, lay Joyce, her lifeless form sending a chill through his veins. John's face drained of all colour as he fell to his knees beside her, desperately searching for any sign of life. His trembling hands brushing against her still-warm body. However, her closed eyes and lack of breath confirmed the unthinkable. She was gone. It was a sight John hoped to never see again.

The kitchen was a mess. Scattered pots and pans continued the picture of a violent altercation. Amongst the smeared and splattered blood, a pool had formed. The scene testified to the magnitude of Joyce's struggle to survive.

A quick scan for clues found nothing to explain what had happened, except…inside the back door lay a distinctive knife. Someone had wiped away a faint streak of blood. This was no ordinary knife, though, and ignoring his instincts, he picked it up for closer examination. The yellow-green wooden handle contained a unique burl pattern that resembled a phoenix. The blade possessed a look and feel that exuded superior style and value. Despite not being an expert, John knew it to be out of place in that kitchen. After carefully restoring the knife to where he found it, he raced next door to raise the alarm and have Josey call the police.

John's mind was abuzz with questions. Obviously, someone had killed Joyce. But why? That knife wasn't Joyce's. Where had it come from? He didn't have answers, nor did he imagine he was the one that could solve this mystery. But as his mind whirred, an overwhelming grief embraced him, and crying led to a deep sobbing.

It was another question that snapped him back to reality, though. Where was Joe? He ran back inside and looked around the rooms, a lump rising in his throat. Joe was nowhere to be seen.

Fear that the police might suspect him and confiscate the time machines hurried him to get out, and fast. Police whistles echoed in the distance, so John rushed to his room and fumbled for the devices, hoping they would work again and transport him to safety.

The dials and watch were stiff, but they moved. As each dial went into place, the whistles grew louder. With just the watch left to set, the plodding sound of running policemen was outside the house.

A constable shouted orders. "You two look for him in that house, and I'll go in here." Before he could knock on Josey's door, she had it open.

"He's in his room, up the stairs on the left,"

John wasn't waiting to find out why she was directing the police towards him. The watch was taking longer than he'd hoped and in haste he fumbled it, losing it under the bed.

A policeman banged on his door. "Open up. This is the police."

John flung the bed at the door to reveal the watch, then pressed his feet against the bed and his back against the wall to keep the door shut. The final setting still needed to be set, and the bedroom door was now banging against the bed as constables pushed harder and harder to get in.

"Got it!" John shouted.

The policemen gave it everything they had, and the door flung open. As their eyes adjusted to a blinding flash of light, they found nothing in the room other than a bed, a small table, and a lamp with a smashed bulb.

FOUR

MURDER MOST STRANGE

Tom didn't know whether to be concerned or laugh, but John's appearance brought the questions thick and fast. "Are you OK? What's with the blood and the old-fashioned gear?"

John fell on his back in the grass, his breathing rapid and his eyes closed.

But Tom wanted answers. "Where have you been? When have you been?"

A few minutes passed before John's eyes opened. "You would not believe what I was doing five minutes ago!" He recounted his past couple of days, as Tom's expression changed from disbelief to utter disgust.

"World War Two!" He gave a look that if they could kill, his friend would have been six feet under. As incensed as he was by John's failure to abide by their agreement, he was just as turned off by his recent lack of oral hygiene. "Ew! Brush your teeth, dude?"

Offended, yet covering his mouth, John gave it back. "Shut it, kid!

I need to wash this blood off. I would love some food and sleep. Oh, and if you have a toothbrush and paste, I'd appreciate it."

No one else was at the cabin, so John could spend the day sleeping and realigning his body clock, after which he sat and chatted without his chin slumping into this chest every five minutes.

"OK, so what's next with the time travelling?" Tom was keen to know if John had any intention of following their previous guidelines.

John explained his immediate desire. "Can I stay here tonight and get a proper sleep before I leave again?"

"I guess so. Please don't snore, though. I can't abide a loud snorer," Tom said. "Do you snore?"

"How do I know? I'm asleep." John spoke in his usual matter-of-fact way. "Did I snore six months ago?"

Tom thought long and hard. "Can't remember."

"I'll take that as a no. Thank You!" John said with smug satisfaction.

After enjoying a meal and some laughs at more of John's stories about the future, not caring how they might affect Tom's life prospects, they settled down to sleep.

John did snore. Tom's memory was well and truly jogged.

Next morning they woke to a gorgeous day. John rose early, ready to embrace the outdoors and found some shorts and a singlet and set off up the road for a run before breakfast. Trees towered overhead, their branches reaching out like gnarled fingers. The fresh scent of pine and damp earth filled the air as the occasional rabbit darted through the underbrush. Peaceful solitude gave him goosebumps as he enjoyed living in the moment.

After running beyond his usual ten minutes, John slowed as a clearing, which overlooked a breath-taking panorama, opened before him. The sun rose over a vast array of colours and countryside, and iced the cake of his morning; a moment of such indescribable beauty that John wondered if even Heaven could beat it. He stood in amazement, basking in its brilliance, until the sun was up and the forest wide awake. There are few sights devoid of sinister elements, offering only serenity, but that morning John discovered perfection, and took it all in.

It was time to head back. On the dusty road once more, a battered old truck trundled towards him. A wave of acknowledgement went up, but something stopped him dead in his tracks. His eyes bulged in disbelief. Dust flew up and obscured his view, but he could see a young boy in the passenger seat who looked the spitting image of Joe. Neither the boy nor the driver appeared to notice him, though.

He sped up to see them for as long as possible, but once the vehicle had passed, it was too fast and left him with nothing but the sound of its clattering engine. John made a mental note of the "1971 West Virginia license plate G104" in case he saw it again.

A hurried run back ended with him bursting into the cabin. "Tom, I'm staying!"

Tom, having clambered out of bed five minutes earlier, raised an eyebrow. "Oh, yeah? Why?"

"I saw the boy from 1941." John couldn't stand still. "At least I think I did, but I need to be sure. And if it is him, my guess is that whoever is with him killed his mother."

"So, you're going to stay here?" Tom looked at John over the rim of his coffee mug.

"Yeah." John took Tom's mug from him and slurped his coffee.

Tom knew the forested area had a sinister history. "Wouldn't it be dangerous to be out here alone if that was Joyce's murderer?"

"True. I need to find somewhere on the edge of town, but nowhere close to my parents' place."

"Now, what about money?" Tom had a gift for making money, but a bigger character flaw in losing it.

"Tom, did you place that bet I mentioned?" John expected he knew the answer.

"Which bet?" Tom looked puzzled.

John looked down. "No way! Don't tell me you forgot!"

Tom smirked. "I had $1,000 lying around and I put it all on Ferdinand to win; which is precisely what he did. I won $17,000. There's only a few thousand left, though."

"You spent it all?" It was John's turn to be annoyed. "Your bender must have been amazing for a sixteen-year-old!" John no longer had the cash reserves he'd planned to enjoy. "I need to make some quick cash," he thought, remembering there were plenty of illegal sports books around town.

"Give me five minutes. I'll be back." He picked up the time machines and, with a few adjustments, there was a flash of light and he'd gone.

Within a mere couple of seconds, John reappeared in the same spot. He stumbled, landing on his feet. After repeated travels in quick succession, he looked around for a few seconds without saying a word, his arms extended as his swaying reduced. With a sigh of relief, he said, "Got 'em!"

"Got what?" Tom looked at the paper in John's hand.

John's eyes gleamed with intent. "A gold mine. An absolute gold mine!"

The crumpled piece of paper contained scribbled notes.

"When did you go to?" Tom looked at his friend with eyes wide and a thrill in his voice. "It's so cool that you fly through time with such little effort."

"Not sure I fly. Not sure what I do, to be honest. I returned home to 2023. It's what I know and there's Internet," John said, unaware that he'd spark Tom's imagination. It took an hour to explain the Internet and to satisfy Tom's incessant curiosity. By the end, John wanted nothing more than to eat brunch and chill.

The morning rolled into the afternoon, and they packed up the few items they needed and headed back to town, ditching the stolen car on the outskirts, and walking the last couple of miles.

"Let's go to the movies, John." Tom had been wanting to watch a movie that had come out a few weeks earlier, Back To The Future.

"Hey, I've seen this one. This is a classic," John responded, trying to be funny. Tom stared blankly, missing the quote from the movie he hadn't seen yet.

Due to a guilty conscience, Tom sighed and coughed up $5,000 for John to place on The White Sox beating The Red Sox 7 to 2 at Fenway Park later that evening. After hanging out, they strolled to the theatre, John reminiscing about past and future shared movie experiences.

Part way through the movie, Tom burst into laughter. No one else laughed. "A classic! Love it! That's what you said." John smiled and returned to his doze.

When the movie ended, John awoke for the fourth time. One previous time, Tom had nudged him because of the extreme snoring. Another, Tom dribbled Coke down his forehead until he stopped.

Tom was buzzing with how the movie's time travel theme tied in with them. John knew what Tom was about to announce publicly. He slapped him hard on the back of the head, at which Tom punched John's arm. A lady passing their aisle murmured, "Kids these days. No respect for their parents." John looked at Tom. "Yes, Junior. No respect!" He spun his head round, stood up, and walked away, faking a look of sheer contempt.

However, the fun ended as a chill ran down John's spine. He

caught sight of a man and a boy leaving the theatre. They were the ones he'd seen in the truck that morning. Outside, the streetlights cast eerie shadows that seemed to follow them. John seized Tom by the arm and quickened his pace, a knot of unease tightening in his gut. But curiosity drove him forward like a relentless beast.

They drew closer, the boy turned, and John's breath caught in his throat as he realised that was Joe. His mind raced. How could this be? He feared that the course of history had changed, with disastrous consequences because of his time travelling shenanigans.

The man turned, catching John's eye. It was a face he did not recognise at first, but contained a fleck of familiarity; a rough-looking character in his twenties. John could not place him, until, unable to contain himself, he called out, "Joe!"

The boy's face revealed recognition of John, but no one said a word.

With Tom behind him, John approached, his hand outstretched in a gesture he hoped would show goodwill. However, before anyone could speak, a fist came out of nowhere and landed squarely on John's jaw, knocking him to the ground. John's senses exploded in a kaleidoscope of pain as he crumpled to the unforgiving pavement.

Tom sprang into action, throwing punches in quick succession and landing several blows. This only resulted in making the guy angrier, his solid frame absorbing the onslaught and retaliating with a heavy blow to Tom's gut.

Tom's face exuded a mix of surprise and instant pain as he also crumpled into a heap on the ground. John struggled to his feet, his vision a swimming haze of stars and confusion. The assailant looked to have noticed something on the ground, because he bent down, picked it up and grabbed the child's arm before taking off at pace, avoiding further interaction and leaving John and Tom behind.

Tom pushed through the pain and pulled himself to his feet; determination etched on his face. He knew he couldn't overpower the man, but he was lightning fast on his feet, and gave chase; his breaths coming in short bursts as he closed on the couple.

At the end of the street, the man pulled the boy into a narrow alley. Tom was about thirty metres back, his heart pounding out of his chest. He slowed, taking a wide approach to the alley, cautious of a potential trap. But as he turned the corner, a flash of light caught his eye, and both were nowhere to be seen.

John was way back. He didn't have Tom's pace, which he put down to his age. By the time he caught up, Tom was still breathing heavily, for although he was fast, he was unfit, and regretted not joining John for that morning jog.

Even as a teen, John loved to give Tom a good ribbing. "You could benefit from my old man's lungs." Tom recognised the glint in John's eye he'd become accustomed to.

Tom gave as good as he got, his playful retort laden with menace. "Watch it, old timer, or I'll slap you and see how you like it." His hand twitched as if poised to strike, only to halt as John turned, sensing someone watching from across the street.

A silent observer lurked in the cloak of darkness. Yet before John could unravel the mystery of the stranger's intent, he took off down a side street, leaving behind a palpable aura of unease. Tom and John looked at each other, unsure whether to follow or ignore him.

"Let him go. We've had enough freaky weird stuff for one day. And besides, I'd better find a place to sleep tonight, Tom." John made his way to the nearest motel and set himself up, while Tom continued home to see if his parents had returned from wherever they'd been for the last three weeks.

The following morning, dawn crept into John's consciousness

with all the urgency of a slug on Xanax; his head throbbing in protest against the unwelcome intrusion of daylight. Time had been at his beck and call, but now it seemed to take control; each passing minute dragging its feet. Yet amidst the sluggish haze of his stupor, a glimmer of anticipation stirred.

The memory of last night's successful wager lingered, promising a windfall of riches waiting to be claimed. With the outcome of the baseball game already foreseen, John's outlook improved, and he ventured off to collect the hefty sum of $80,000.

His confidence wasn't lacking as he kept $10,000 aside to hide in his room. Such an irresistible opportunity for another sure thing beckoned with the allure of an even greater fortune. $70,000 went on The Indians beating The Yankees 4 to 3 in Cleveland the following afternoon; the first of a doubleheader.

Despite Joe having disappeared again, John wasn't ready to leave 1986, especially with such a large sum of money coming his way. Instead, he wandered the streets, looking to indulge himself. The smell of grilled burgers wafted through the air, drawing John towards a familiar haven of comfort: Burger King. With a Whopper in hand, he savoured a small pleasure amidst the uncertainty of temporal flux, before returning to his former sanctuary, the musty motel.

He checked out and found an upscale first floor hotel suite. Satisfied and sighing, he surrendered to the embrace of the couch, content knowing that, for now at least, all was right with the world, and drifted off to sleep.

Something jolted him awake, interrupting a troop of lavender haired grannies in his dream chasing him through a maternity ward armed with knitting needles and bingo cards. Grateful to find himself clothed in the waking world, darkness enveloped his room, with a single streetlamp casting spooky shadows. As he stumbled forward in the dim light to relieve the mounting pressure on his bladder, he couldn't help but wonder if his subconscious had taken a detour through the Twilight Zone.

Almost to the toilet bowl, he realised he had only peed once since his travels began. He knew his prostate wasn't yet the size of a pea, so what might be the cause? He had no recollection of what happened during the time jumps and considered the possibility that the corridors of time have cubicles that supernaturally relieve the need. Despite his theory, he needed to relieve the need now, so set himself in place.

Through the open bathroom window, the sight of two men caught his eye. One was well-dressed, and the other wore a hoody and stood with his legs bowed. As the seconds passed, John daydreamed about who they were and what they were discussing. His staring continued until he realised one had turned his head and appeared to be looking in his direction. Fearful of being spotted, he dropped to his knees, forgetting where he was and what he had been doing. Relief hit him as he remembered he'd shaken out the final dregs of his business a few seconds before.

With regained composure, and having washed his hands, he stepped out onto the street, unsure which direction he wanted to go, or even what the time was. The sense of time had become jumbled with his watch still showing 2023 time. A teenager came to the rescue, helping him set it to 7.06pm.

More grounded in the present now, he still experienced pangs of guilt, burdened by Joyce's violent death. As a result, the beckoning of simple comfort lured him towards another greasy burger. And back at his hotel room, whilst wondering what his old friend was up to, John drifted into a food coma.

* * *

Tom's Uncle Phil had often recanted the story of his biggest heist, robbing what was now the Harding Estate. With heart pounding, Tom made it up towards that house to emulate the feat, his mind racing with a mixture of fear and excitement. He had cased the joint for weeks. Now, with the thrill that comes from choosing the richest house in town, this would be his big heist.

Through the gates he slipped, like a shadow, careful not to raise any alarms. The moon provided little light, hidden behind a thick layer of clouds, giving Tom the perfect cover to move undetected towards the house.

Once there, he paused, listening for signs of life. With nothing on the radar, he handled the security by shorting the alarm system, just as his uncle taught him, and once inside, accessing the hidden CCTV VCR and shredding the tape.

Inside was not as he had imagined, as astounding opulence clashed with lavish décor in a catastrophe of colours and patterns, hinting at tasteless design skills. Undeterred at being underwhelmed by tackiness, he pressed on, listening to the echo of his footsteps, pretty sure no one would hear. But exploring each room increased a sense of foreboding, like a whisper of unseen danger lurking in the shadows.

Unsure he would find anything portable and valuable enough to steal, he entered the ballroom and discovered the treasures he sought. Stood still and gawking at the gold-trimmed décor for a moment, he nodded in appreciation.

With a quickening pulse, he zeroed in on the golden candelabras. But about to grab his prize, his triumph was short-lived. The unmistakable sound of cars pulling into the drive shattered the silence, followed by the front door opening.

A jolt of panic shot through Tom as he realised there was nowhere to go. A scan of the room found long velvet curtains in front of the floor-to-ceiling windows. Without a second thought, he darted behind them and cracked open a window to ready his escape.

From outside the room, the footsteps drew closer, and an argument began between two men. Tom's heart raced as they walked into the ballroom and turned on the chandelier lighting. His fate hung in the balance with every movement, poised on the edge of discovery.

The heavy drapes muffled the heated exchange, but Tom's curiosity got the better of him, and he stole a glance through a slender gap, catching their reflections in the grand, gilded mirror. Every gesture, every furrowed brow, etched in stark clarity. The older man, veins pulsating with agitation, clashed with the steely resolve of his younger counterpart, who looked determined to find something.

Tom contemplated slipping away, but a faint noise from the doorway seized the arguers' attention. A sudden silence enveloped the room, gripping them all, before the thunderous crack of a gunshot shattered the tension. The older man crumpled to the floor, blood pooling around him. The young man looked down in horror before turning towards the shot's origin. A look of dread consumed him.

As disaster gripped everyone else, Tom seized his chance. Adrenaline coursed through his veins as he exited the open window, moving each limb with the care you'd take the first time you hold a baby. Desperate to escape the nightmare, he shuddered as another gunshot, followed by a cacophony of clattering, emanated from within the house. With quiet haste, he tip-toe-ran down the driveway, concentrating hard to contain his fear through steady breathing. His mind reeled, considering the argument, the gunshot, and the body, as he ran for ten minutes straight.

Slick with sweat and thoughts consumed by panic, the last thing he wanted was to be alone. He needed to find John, and on route to the motel, he did.

This John was sixteen. "What's going on, Tom?" He eyed Tom up and down with a disconcerting look. "You seen a ghost?"

Tom took several long deep breaths, raising a finger to indicate he needed a minute. Once able to speak, he said, "It's a long story."

"I've got time." John's gaze didn't waver.

Tom hesitated before fessing up about the break-in, argument, and gunshot.

John listened; his expression unreadable. After a long, awkward silence, he said, "We need to go to the police. This is serious."

Tom's eyes widened in fear. "No way!" His voice weak with worry. "You didn't hear that gunshot!" His voice grew louder with exasperation. "I don't want to end up like that old dude. And besides, I wasn't there playing tiddly winks. I was robbing the place. No one will believe me, and I'll become suspecto numero uno."

"Yeah, probably." John conceded.

The two friends walked and Tom calmed down. It wasn't long, though, before his memory riled him up again. After a moment's hesitation, unsure whether to bring it up, he gave into the nagging desire.

"I saw Alice on the bus the other day," he said as casually as possible.

John's expression changed, and his stride became irregular. "Yeah?"

"She wasn't alone either." He glanced across at John, keen to see his expression.

John cleared his throat. "Who was she with? Sharon and Karen?"

Tom probed further. "No. A guy that was making moves on my girl."

"Funny. I rode the same bus as Alice a few days ago. I didn't see anyone making any moves."

Tom raised an eyebrow. "Why was your arm round her? An indelible source informed me that you were on a date."

John leaned in close, his eyes narrowing. "Is that right? You can tell your indelible source to drop dead. Who would tell you that?"

Tom avoided John's gaze. "I can't tell you, dude. That wouldn't be cool."

John's voice grew louder and higher pitched. "Not cool? What's not cool is someone talking trash behind my back. Give me a name, man!"

"You wouldn't believe me if I told you."

John came right into Tom's face. "Try me!"

Tom paused and scratched the back of his head as his eyes and lips screwed up, before he turned to John and said, "You did. You came back from the future and reminisced about the entire episode, and we saw you on the bus."

John backed off and stared at Tom. "What kind of weird shit is that, dude? You were at the magic mushies again!"

"You wanted the truth." Tom's head dropped. "So, I told you the truth. Your problem is you can't handle the truth."

"You're stonewalling." John stormed off in frustration.

Tom shouted after him, "You had a choice to make between your friend and his girl. You chose the girl."

Alone again, a deeper depression enfolded Tom than before. He hoped the older John would be more understanding, so continued to his motel.

* * *

John left instructions at the motel directing Tom to him, lazing on a grease-stained couch. Tom recounted the evening's events, after which John apologised for his younger self and empathised with the stress of witnessing a murder. The breaking and entering, though, is where he drew the line. "Sometimes when you do bad, karma slaps you hard."

"Had I known…" Tom stopped himself. "You know what? The man I saw in the house, the one that did not get shot, I think he was the same guy we saw in the shadows during the alley incident."

John turned pale. "That's spooky! I'm not sure he was watching us so much as them. Why, though?" He paced the room before tripping over a rug. "Who put that there?" The jolt cleared his thoughts. "Are you up for playing detective, my friend?" The idea they could investigate a murder appealed to them both.

"Sure. Why not? I don't do school much, so I'm free for an adventure." Tom laughed. "Even though you're an old dude now, it'll feel like we're the Hardy Boys."

"You, Tom, have to be the only impartial person who can actually tell what happened in that house tonight."

Tom waited for him to continue, but John said nothing. "So?"

"So, I will go back to that alley and have a little chat with the young man." John spoke with authority. "But not right now. I'm tired. That is the beauty of time travel, my friend." With a broad smile, he strode off to bed. "Time waits for me."

FIVE

PRIVATE INVESTIGATION

"That's our number one on this week's Billboard One Hundred." The radio woke John blaring out Peter Gabriel's Sledgehammer. A Dire Straits medley followed, which was perfect as he was a huge fan of the eighties, while Tom was still finding his way in music. The opening lyrics of Private Investigations hit home. "It's a mystery to me. The game commences." Filled with a healthy dose of trepidation, both looked forward to their investigative exploits.

Right now, though, it was time for John to find out what information he could gain from speaking with the young man Tom saw in the Harding house that night. He pulled out the devices, set his course, and gave it a little shake.

Wednesday 30th July 1986, 9.34pm, Hometown

A hundred metres down the side street, he waited, reflecting on how convoluted his travels had become. He was now literally in two places at once.

A minute later, a tall young man ran towards him. As soon as John saw him under a streetlight, he knew who it was. "Brian? Is that you?"

The young man slowed and, after a few more strides, stopped, before looking straight at John with a semblance of recognition. Confused, John turned his head to the side as his eyes narrowed. "How do you know me?"

The young man's reply blew John's mind.

"If only!" he said.

John, overcome with grief, flashed back to the photo in which he first saw Joyce. The thought hit him like a thunderbolt, though, that perhaps Brian had some connection with her. But when he looked up to ask, no one was there.

The entire episode should have provided answers, but only created more questions, so he returned to Tom empty.

Friday 1st August 1986, 8.17am, Hometown

Not wanting to go into detail, he dismissed what had happened. Instead, he focused on something more uplifting.

"Listen Tom." John couldn't help but grin. "Before we do anything, I'm heading off to claim my winnings."

Tom raised an eyebrow. "Shouldn't you check the score first, old man? Make sure you've actually won?"

John waved a dismissive hand. "Nah, I've got this. Trust me." And off he swaggered to the sports book, strutting through the door like a peacock on steroids, and demanded the manager, Jungo Jim, see him. Confident about the size of his winnings, he presented his winning ticket and waited for the Jungo's response.

Jungo burst into laughter and handed back the ticket. "You already have your winnings. The Yankees beat the Indians 4 to 3."

John's face drained of colour. "That can't be right!" His voice softened as he walked away. "I swear that score was different." John made his apologies for his earlier arrogance and left, displaying a lot less plumage than on arrival.

Outside, Tom could see that John's face indicated failure. "You didn't win, did you?"

John shook his head and looked down. "Nope. Something's not right. Father Time is getting off watching me squirm. And it's not the first time that something changed since 2023. This time travel thing isn't easy."

Tom's eyes widened. "What do you mean? What happened before?"

"I had my wallet," John grumbled. "It was in my back pocket when I returned from 2023. Now, where's it gone? These timelines keep messing with me. Aargh! I always said time travel was such a bunch of bollocks!"

Tom stared in wonder, allowing John to let off steam. "I have no idea what you mean by that 'bollocks' comment, nor why you used such a British-ism. But please don't give an explanation, nor a demo."

Together, they made their way back to John's suite, picking up a free paper in the foyer. John flung the paper on the table and went to the bathroom. When he returned, he'd clearly done some thinking on the throne, calmed his nerves, and reconsidered his position. There was still $10,000, but a sense of impoverishment now overcame him. Too much time must have transpired, he theorised, and his actions somehow changed the result. With a new bunch of scores, he would place bets he couldn't have already affected.

"OK, here goes again. Give me the devices. I may need to find more results," John said with the determination his mother illustrated when asking his father to wash the dishes; wishy-washy but ultimately wanting a result.

Within a few seconds, he'd flashed, returned and was ready to head out the door to give it another go. $8,500 was to go on the exact scores he'd researched. The accumulator of the four events came to odds of 600 to 1. If he won, he'd be up for winnings of $5.1 million.

The lady behind the counter was adamant. "We cannot take that bet."

"Call Jungo. He'll take it." John gambled that Jungo's desire to humiliate him further would work in his favour.

As he walked in, Jungo's broad smile indicated John was right. "Well, I'll give you this. You've got some big kahunas, buddy! You have next to no chance of even one of these results being accurate. But four? You make me laugh. If you win, you can have this gold tooth as a memento." His mouth opened wide to reveal the capping on a molar, plus a terrible case of halitosis.

"I'll hold you to that," John said.

Back at the hotel, Tom was eager to show him the free paper. "John. John!" His voice grew louder. "You need to come and see this."

Brutal Murder Shocks Local Community, read the headline.

The only information we have is that someone killed James Andersen, a car salesman in town. Police have no one in cuffs yet, but they're on the hunt for two people as two sets of bloodied fingerprints littered the crime scene. Rumours swirled like a tornado in heat concerning who might have done it.

"Two suspects!" Tom looked at John in disbelief. "They must be talking about the guy I saw and the gunman."

With the murder in the news, they sensed a responsibility to disclose the truth. "Come on, Tom." John wanted to do some digging. "This must be the talk of the town. Let's chat with a few locals and see what they say. Perhaps someone can give us a lead."

They approached a group of men outside a bar, smoking and talking in hushed tones.

"Hey, fellas. You hear about that murder?" John asked.

One man nodded; his face grim. "Yeah, we heard. Being rich doesn't save you if your number's up, does it?"

Tom leaned in. "Who would have done such a thing?"

Uncertain looks between the men surprised John, before one said, "Rumour has it this was a hit. That guy, Andersen, owed some bad people some big money. Must have caught up with him."

John raised an eyebrow. "Bad people, huh? Like who?"

The man shrugged. "I don't know, man. You don't wanna get mixed up in that kinda thing. And if I knew, do you think I'd be telling you? That'd get me shot."

They continued down the street and overheard snippets of conversations from shopkeepers and passersby. Some speculated that it was a case of mistaken identity, while others whispered about a love triangle gone wrong.

The murder shook the town, leaving everyone on edge.

"We need to go back to the house and take a look for ourselves." John was serious, but Tom was less keen to return to this house of horrors after the previous night's trauma. After a brief period of consideration, and realising John would be there, his trepidation eased. Unable to investigate right away because police still surrounded the area, they agreed to return once night fell, and left for a snooze.

A little after midnight, they approached a deserted street. Streetlamps flickered, casting eerie shadows on the sidewalk, and thick clouds obscured the moon again, making it hard to see anything.

They gained access through a neighbour's garden to avoid the yellow police tape and police parked outside the main gate.

After scaling the wall, and hauling Tom over behind him, John entered the garden. They had remembered to each bring a flashlight, which now came in useful, as an eerie silence and intense darkness made it difficult to traverse dense foliage undetected.

"Do you have the gloves I asked you to bring, Tom?" John wasn't keen to leave fingerprints.

Tom fumbled in his backpack. "This is all I could find."

"You are killing me!" John tried to suppress his laughter.

"Shhhh!" Tom's embarrassment was obvious as he handed over a pair of woollen mittens.

"Great couple of crime fighters we make." John put them on while shaking his head. "I'm meant to be a cat burglar. I feel more like a kitten."

They approached a side window, avoiding creaky wooden planks on the porch. Filled with an intoxicating mixture of excitement and fear, they jimmied open the window and climbed inside. The interior contained an ominous mix of stale air and something else that they couldn't quite identify. At least no one was home, so they could relax a little. John entered the ballroom, the light outside casting eerie shadows through the ornate chandelier. Mixed with reflections in the gilded mirror, a thousand eyes seemed to watch their every move. Tom followed close behind, his senses on high alert, the slightest noise making him jump.

"The shot came from over there." Tom's arm pointed in the direction of the doorway.

"Why are there no evidence markers over there?" John surveyed the doorway. "The police don't seem to know what they're doing." His light shone into nooks and crannies, as he scoured the room for clues.

Tom's heart raced as he approached the spot where Andersen fell. They tried not to disturb the crime scene too much, stepping around the pool of congealed blood.

The scene had changed from the one Tom remembered. The room was a complete mess. Overturned furniture and shattered glass littered the floor, which contained areas of blood-stained marble.

"Come look at these." Tom pointed at bloodied footprints leading from the body's location out towards the hallway. "I wonder what the story is behind them."

John walked over to look. "I have no idea, dude. Although I am getting a strange feeling of déjà vu."

They performed a thorough search for other signs that would give them an edge over the Police investigation.

They whispered few words, as experiencing a murder scene freaked them both. Trying to piece together what had happened was tough. They tossed theories around, but nothing seemed to fit the evidence.

Despite the tension, John couldn't help himself. "I feel like I'm in a time-travelling movie. But instead of a Delorean, I have mittens."

Tom rolled his eyes and pretended to laugh along. "I half expect to see some clue or recognise some object out of the corner of my eye that will solve the complete mystery."

"Wait! What's that?" John noticed something in the middle of a mess of papers. An open cupboard revealed an old, forgotten piece of paper, which he recognised having seen a few days earlier. It took a few seconds, but he realised it was the flier on his work's classifieds board. With mitten-impaired hands, he folded it away in his pocket.

Tom had seen enough and pulled on John's coat to leave. However, turning to retrace their steps, they heard the front door open. A flashlight shone inside the foyer and a loud voice echoed through the empty house, "Police! Who's in here?"

The policemen's footsteps approached. Both of them were right beside the window, so slipped out undetected and followed the perimeter of the building, before taking their chances and running for the neighbour's wall.

They cleared the neighbour's garden and rounded the corner. The exhilaration of avoiding the police poured through their veins.

Tom couldn't help himself. "You know, John, I think this outlaw life suits you."

John chuckled. "I've always had a rebellious streak. I just hid it as a kid."

They strategised their next move as they walked back to the hotel. "Let's find that shadowy guy," Tom said.

Next day, the local paper headline read *Have You Seen This Man?* The story contained the picture of a man in his mid-twenties named Brian.

Police considered him to be the number one suspect. He was the nephew of Steve Harding, the owner of the property, and lived at the same address. The article explained Steve was out of town and his wife, Jane Harding, a well-known socialite, had been at a public meeting at the town hall. Brian had reportedly, from an eyewitness account, run from the house, but had now disappeared without a trace. Police requested that anyone knowing the whereabouts of Brian should not approach him but call 911.

"That is him!" Tom stared at the photo. "That's the guy in the shadows by the alley. The same guy that was at the house that night."

John had focused his attention on Joe that night. A glimpse was all he'd seen of the shadowy figure across the road. There was a familiarity about Brian, though, which bugged him.

They still felt a strong responsibility to exonerate an innocent man. How to do that? They had no clue. Tom's conscience pulled him one way and self-preservation the other. Self-interest won over in the end, and he told John there would be no police confession. To move forward, John found the newspaper article's author and tried to glean some leads.

Paula Atherton was a young journalist with a keen eye for a great story. She would jump into it before anyone else could. Within minutes of the police being informed of James' death, she was at the scene. John tracked her down to the paper's offices where she was hard at work collating more details about the latest information regarding the murder.

"Sorry." Paula looked up at John as he approached her desk. She knew what he wanted. "I can't let you know my sources. The police will find Brian. He is almost certainly the killer. Both the cops and my primary source, who came with impeccable credentials, tell me off the record that they know Brian is guilty."

"What if I told you I have a source who witnessed the murder?" Paula discarded all distractions and sat upright, turning her head to hear every word. "He will only talk with you on the condition of complete anonymity."

"And you are?" Paula jumped up out of her seat.

"You can call me John." He offered a hand to shake.

"A pleasure to meet you, John" She shook his hand and smiled. "I'm Paula. You know I'll need proof they were present, right?"

"Trust me. You'll have your proof." With that, he left to find Tom.

Tom was waiting back in the hotel room. "You can tell your story without getting nabbed by the police." John considered this to be a stroke of genius, which he was proud to have devised.

Tom's response was positive, yet guarded. "I will not reveal my identity to this woman. I don't know her or trust her."

John arranged for Tom to call Paula from a public phone booth.

"What evidence do you have that you witnessed the murder?" Paula began. "And what were you doing there, anyway?"

"I know where the first shot came from." Tom's confidence, as he detailed what he saw, seemed to gain Paula's trust. That changed when he said, "I was there to rob the place. The house would likely be full of antiques and silverware worth good money."

"Why should I believe someone that is so dishonest?" Paula did not hold back.

Tom thought before responding. "Because the victim and that innocent guy both deserve the truth to be known."

Paula played a hunch and listened to Tom's story, taking notes, and asking questions. By the end, he'd convinced her he was telling the truth.

"This changes things. If what you've told me is true, it also makes me question the credibility and motivation of my source." Paula was already typing up the story. "Keep your eyes on tomorrow's paper."

Tom was relieved and John shook his hand, in awe of the bravery his teenage friend had shown.

The following morning, they brimmed with anticipation as they picked up the paper and searched for the headline that would exonerate Brian. Front page, page 2, page 3—nothing. Panic set in as they combed through every article, each passing moment intensifying their desperation. But amidst the sea of print, there was no trace of Paula Atherton.

John trembled as he dialled Paula's desk. At the sound of an unfamiliar voice on the other end, words tumbled from his mouth.

"May I speak with Paula, please?" John's voice quivered with urgency.

"Sorry, she's no longer with us. Can I assist you?" The reply was cold and clinical.

A wave of dread washed over John as he pressed for more information. "What happened? I spoke with her yesterday about the Andersen case. Do you have any idea how I can reach her?"

But silence stonewalled his inquiry, the curt response offering no solace. Frustration boiled within as he hung up.

As the truth sank in, John's mind raced with unanswered questions. What forces had conspired to silence Paula? Was it coercion, corruption, or something far more sinister?

They doubted their amateurish sleuthing skills had any more to offer.

John did, however, have one last roll of the dice. Ever since finding himself as a grown man in 1986, the palpable excitement of a moment of serendipity had grown within. Each passing day, he yearned to encounter a particular somebody.

SIX

ULTERIOR MOTIVE

As a teen, John had fantasised about his French teacher, Mademoiselle Laurent. For him, her age had not detracted from her lustrous chestnut hair, which fell in gentle waves around her shoulders, and captivating hazel eyes that sparkled with warmth. She was a boyhood crush who had once been a police detective, so he saw two good reasons to make contact.

When John mentioned his idea, Tom was keen to watch him try it on with his fantasy older woman, now as a younger woman.

"That will fill my entertainment quota for the week and relieve the stress of the whole situation," Tom responded. "Let's find her."

John had stalked her as a teen, so knew where she lived. But the plan was to bump into her in a shop or the street and come up with a conversation starter.

They came across her walking around town, so Tom egged John on to approach her. But he only became aggravated by Tom's incessant prodding, his nose hairs tingling, as his nostrils flared in anger; an idiosyncrasy of his. He knew how to meet women, but when the time came to make his move, his teenage angst returned, and his jelly-like legs wobbled. And to add insult to injury, he lost sight of Mlle Laurent.

"Now look what you've …"

"Bonjour, Tom." A soft French accent came from behind them.

John turned as her delicate fragrance wafted his way. He could feel the heat sweep into his face, as her scent transported him back forty years.

"Close your mouth," Tom whispered. "Bonjour, Mademoiselle. This is my friend John."

"Enchante monsieur. Have we met before? You look familiar, I think."

John tried hard to compose himself. "I don't believe we have. A woman with such finesse and beauty would be unforgettable. And I don't think I could forget someone as unforgettable as you is…I mean are."

It was now her turn to blush, as Tom dug John in the side, encouraging him to continue the conversation before she walked away. John blurted out, "Oh, er, umm, are you Mlle Laurent? Tom has told me all about you."

This only caused a sharp fist into John's left kidney to produce a muffled, "Mmmmm!"

Mlle Laurent watched with interest as John grappled to find the right words. "I mean, he has told me how much he has enjoyed his French under you. U-under your teaching, that is."

Tom rolled his eyes and walked off.

A smirk grew across Mlle Laurent's face as she responded, "You two are funny. You have made me laugh. Bien."

"Tom told me you used to be a policewoman."

"Oui. I did." With a cheeky smile, she added, "And I still have the uniform."

John's eyes glazed over, before Tom had to return to John's side and pull on the edge of his coat.

Back from cuckoo-dreamland, John said, "Cool. Maybe you could show me sometime. But for right now, I was wondering if you might be interested in helping with our investigation."

"I don't have time for anything related to police work anymore."

"It's about the murder in the Harding house mentioned in the paper. We have inside information that the prime suspect is innocent, but we need help to prove it." John had regained full control of his mouth, plus the palpitations that threatened to expose more than just his racing pulse.

"Why not go to the police?"

"It's not that simple, mademoiselle," Tom said. "We were there, but not legally, if you catch my drift. The wrong place at kind of the right time to see that Brian Harding was not the killer. We didn't, however, see who did fire the shot."

"Mon Dieu! You were both there? What were you doing there? On second thoughts, no, don't tell me."

"What's with the we?" John was not keen to be considered dumb enough to witness a murder because of criminal activities of his own. "I am helping clear an innocent man. Never include me with you at the house. Thank you very much! Not at the time of the murder, anyway."

"Have you been to the scene since the murder?" Mlle Laurent's jaw dropped in disbelief. "Are you crazy? You will be the next suspects! Why did you go back?"

John detailed their story, his sincerity illustrating the desire to see justice served. He confessed it was a bit of an adventure. Mlle Laurent listened. It tweaked an acute sensibility that had solved crimes before, and she was keen to revisit her detective past to aid the duo. She suggested the trio meet back at her place later that afternoon. John's mind reverted to his teenage years for a few seconds, imagining how he would deal with being inside her house.

Tom and John knocked on the front door at 4pm and Mlle Laurent answered the door wearing a figure-hugging outfit that made John gulp so loud he was sure everyone heard. She welcomed them in, and John strolled inside, followed by Tom, eyes glued to John's every move.

"John, call me Marie, s'il te plait." The subtlety of her perfume teased him as he hung on her every word.

In responding, he hoped to sound confident, but said, "Mais bien sur, Marie. Oh, you can um … call me… John."

"That's what she said." Tom said, rolling his eyes and kneeing John, stronger than intended, in his left thigh.

John yelped in pain, whilst laughing at the absurdity of Tom quoting Michael Scott from The Office twenty years before it had even aired.

Marie was ready with food. "No soup for you, pizza man!" she said, as Tom consumed an entire pizza, leaving John the tomato soup.

John couldn't help himself. "He's kinda weedy. The carbs will do him good."

Once fed, Marie settled them down to business. "What have we got? Who was involved? Brian Harding, James Andersen and at least one other person who Brian recognised. This is our only clue right now. We need to find a motive and that may lead us towards identifying the killer. For this, we need to get to know who these people are and were. Also, is there any physical evidence? None at this moment, but maybe we will find some along the way. Let's see what we can learn at the Library about the Hardings and the Andersens. Ready?"

The walk to Marie's car was eventful. Initially, John had a limp. But as soon as Tom said, "Hey, someone's behind that tree." The limp vanished. John lunged at Tom, who yelped in pain, as a punch to his belly winded him so thoroughly that it was ten minutes before he could allay Marie's fears, while she repeatedly asked, "Are you alright, Tom?"

"He tripped. I caught him. He'll be fine. Won't you, buddy?" John ruffled Tom's hair whilst scowling at him. "Let's be careful out there. OK?" To move things along before any further comments exited Tom's mouth, John said, "To the Batmobile!"

At the library, they approached the main desk to request access to the microfiche machine for studying newspaper articles.

"Is there anything in particular that you are searching for?" the librarian inquired.

John noticed her name badge. "Well Jane, yes there is. Anything and everything about the local Andersen and Harding families and their business dealings."

The short stocky lady stood for a second, not moving a muscle as the suggestion of a scowl curled on her face. "Come with me," she said, directing them towards the machines. About to walk away, her finger came up to her chin. "If you find anything, let me know and I will see if I can aid you further."

They shared two machines and scoured the archives. Tom insisted he could work best on his own and so Marie and John collaborated.

"I have something," Tom said after five minutes. "It's that manor house. Jane Harding purchased it in 1979 and the next thing I found was a wedding announcement of Jane Jackson to Steve Harding in May 1979. They don't seem to have had any kids yet."

Marie wanted to know, "Is there any mention of Steven Harding prior to 1979?"

"No," Tom replied. "I found that my Uncle Phil was in trouble with the law in 1970 for car theft. Police said he had an accomplice, but no mention of them ever catching anyone else. I've always liked Uncle

Phil. Taught me everything I know about life."

A few minutes later, Marie spotted an advert for a car yard with James Andersen's name mentioned. And with a bit more digging, his business partner was Steven Harding.

After a two-hour session, several pages of scrawl on screwed up paper were on Tom's desk and Marie had accumulated a similar amount of immaculate typography on perfectly aligned pages. It was time to call it a day.

As they approached the exit, Jane asked if they'd made progress.

"Very much so," Marie said. "With our findings, I think we have some promising avenues to explore."

"Is that right?" Jane took a step towards them. "Allow me to introduce myself."

"Jane Harding, I presume?" Marie made a beeline for her. "Do you mind if we ask you some questions?"

"Yes, I do mind." Jane's tone changed. "We have been through a lot recently and I don't know what you hope to find, but we are a decent, hard-working family. It is strange that you are investigating us. What is it for, anyway?"

Tom spoke up. "We know Brian Harding is innocent and intend to find the actual killer."

Jane looked stunned, before she turned and walked away, leaving the trio to exit the library into a beautiful summer evening. Tom lived nearby so went home, which left the middle-agers alone.

"Why don't we leave my car here and stroll back to my place, John?" Marie's carefree proposition took John by surprise, causing his heart to skip a beat, and he agreed without hesitation.

Side by side, their steps kept harmonious time, as they strolled along serene streets; the sweet scent of flowers adding to the ambience. Conversation was light-hearted and their laughter mingled with a gentle breeze rustling through the trees. On occasion, they paused in awe, captivated by the allure of an enchanting house or well-manicured garden.

"How do you like them apples?" John asked as he picked some low hanging fruit.

"I'm more of a plums kind of girl myself."

John turned, looked at Marie, and his lower jaw dropped as his mind drifted off on a tangent. "Whoopsie daisies!" A paving stone tripped him up.

"What did you say? Did you say whoopsie daisies?" Marie said with a giggle.

"No, nobody says whoopsie daisies anymore. I said 'Ooh these crazies.' I was talking about whoever put that damn paver there." John's face was the picture of pure innocence.

"You did say whoopsie daisies." Marie slapped him on the arm, and they burst into laughter.

Once they rounded the corner into Marie's street, it was as if time had slowed to a crawl, while the sky had painted itself with hues of orange and pink. The gentle hum of laughter and smooth jazz drifted from homes, as they inhaled the mesmerising ambience. With a shared smile and lingering glance, they stood motionless yet relaxed on her doorstep, the subtle porch light adding a touch of tranquillity. Their words left open the potential for future magical evenings as they bid goodnight.

John walked away, reliving his surreal experience over and over. A few cherished moments that captured the magic and possibility of a blossoming relationship. It was at this point he realised there was a long walk back to his place but it was worth it, having fulfilled a fantasy. The sky transformed into a tapestry of twinkling stars with a slither of a moon, all of which lit his journey of endless side streets.

Twenty minutes in and he crossed the street before letting a car pass. John resumed his stride, his mind still in a dream-like haze. But in that fleeting moment, an unexpected force yanked him back with sudden violence. A car, invisible in the darkness, emerged from the shadows, racing past without headlights. The screech of tyres piercing the tranquil night. His heart leapt out of his chest as he realised it missed him by inches. Time seemed to slow as the car sped on, its blurred form in the distance a stark reminder of the close call. John's pulse pounded in his ears, with adrenaline pumping through his veins. Flat on his back and trembling, the gravity of the situation sank in.

After several minutes of lying on the sidewalk and recovering, his mind cleared, and he looked around to see who had saved him. There was no one in sight. For the rest of the walk, John couldn't help but look over his shoulder every few seconds.

A wave of gratitude washed over him as he unlocked the door to his room. Exhausted on the bed, he took a moment to reflect on the night's events, and within a minute, was away with the fairies.

The new day began with a loud knocking, which startled John out of his slumber. The clock showed 9.57am, at which he realised, "That was one heck of a deep sleep!"

On opening the door, the hotel manager beckoned him like a dog. "I need you out. You have five minutes."

Taken aback, but not too fussed, John was out of there and on the street. Well, sort of. He went next door to the Cafe Deluxe for breakfast. One minute later, he was back on the street. They refused to serve him. When he tried to get a taxi, they all drove by with no customers inside.

"What is going on? What is wrong with you people?"

He called Marie, who picked him up and took him to her place.

As they drove up to the house, the front door was open, but Marie knew she had locked it before leaving. Who might they find inside? After searching the entire house, they found no one.

John turned to Marie. "Someone must be sending a message. But who and why?"

Marie's Gallic temperament came to the fore. "I will not stand by and allow someone to intimidate us. I have no idea who is playing silly buggers, but I will find out and make them pay. Our investigations must be heading in the right direction. I will not take this lying down, John. We will sort this out. If I wasn't out to help before, I sure as hell am now!"

John was so impressed by Marie's forceful persona that he missed his cue to agree. At that moment, everything about her mesmerised him.

"Well? Say something John. What do you think?"

He smiled, awoke from his dazed state, and fumbled for words. "Er, Oh. Yes. Well, naturally, I fully, Marie. Of course. I am complete agreeing." After appearing to have less grasp of the English language than a newt, he formed a coherent sentence. "What are silly buggers? Where did you hear that?"

"Je ne sais pas. I do not know. On my travels somewhere. Why? Is it not English?"

"Depends on who the silly buggers are." John never had much success making women laugh, but on this occasion, his joke hit the mark.

"You are a funny man, and cute with it." Marie looked into John's eyes before something through the window behind him distracted her. "One minute. I will be back." She walked out the front door.

To John's dismay, he watched as, from behind the tree across the road, a teenage boy appeared and ran down the street at great speed.

Marie turned and walked back inside. "Oh, that boy! Makes me so annoyed. My private life is mine. I do not expect my students to stalk me. Stupid Boy! Sorry, John. Ha! John. That's his name too! What a coincidence. Now, where were we?"

"I'd better be going, Marie. I wouldn't want you to confuse my namesake with me."

Marie ran her finger down John's arm as he turned to leave. "What are you talking about? You just have the same name."

But John was too embarrassed to stay. "See you tomorrow."

SEVEN

UNEXPECTED DANGER

The approach to the library enveloped a view that made them stand and stare, admiring the impressive architectural masterpiece, tall and elegant, on the edge of the town's precinct. Its grand façade and large glass windows were a testimony to a local family's generosity. They provided a sizeable donation for its construction twenty years earlier, and the patriarch's name was emblazoned across the entrance - The Joe Jackson Memorial Library.

Inside, the distinctive tones of Jane Harding met them. "You do not have the right to enter this building. Now leave."

"This is a public library, Mrs. Harding. You cannot tell us to leave." Marie walked straight past her and carried on to the public records section. John followed in sheer admiration.

He searched for information about the hotel and Marie about the café. It wasn't until they looked at business records that a pattern formed. Both businesses were owned by a holding company that also owned and whose primary address was a large warehouse in the industrial park not far from the centre of town. A notable owner of the holding company, Jackson Holdings, was one Jane Harding.

"We need to go and see that warehouse, John." Marie had all she wanted and was ready to pack up when two local policemen arrived and asked them to leave. With no argument, they obliged.

Outside, on a cozy bench under the shade of a tall oak tree, providing protection from the scorching summer sun, they huddled, their heads ticking over with ideas. With hushed voices, their faces showed a mix of determination and excitement as they figured how to gain access to the warehouse.

"You know we are being watched, don't you, Marie?" John was aware of the ever-present gaze of Jane Harding peering down upon them from her librarian's seat. "Let's give her a show. I wanna see her reaction."

For the next five minutes, the couple pointed at their papers and back at the library. With exaggerated gestures, the volume of their voices rose and echoed through the precinct. The air of excitement grew until they stood and hurried to their car, as if to be in a hurry to get somewhere important.

"Is she looking, John?"

"Oh, yeah!" he said. "So much so that there is a line of agitated people queuing at the reception desk."

"She is worth investigating. I have a hunch we will find something of interest when we get to that warehouse. We may be on the road to finding our killer."

John wanted to know, "Are we going in the front door during business hours or the back door after hours?"

"There will be no great welcoming committee. So, best we make our entry in secret. I am no longer a cop, so I won't be requesting a warrant before performing a search." Both eyebrows raised, showing she meant business.

"Think we'll need some expert assistance," John said. "And I know just the guy to help."

Tom's skills in the dark art of breaking and entering were phenomenal, but he had never taken on a commercial building before. John thought that, if nothing else, this would stretch his skills to the next level.

In the shadows of the city, they set plans and acquired blueprints. Tom's confidence surged as he eyed the warehouse, his mind calculating entry strategies with precision. His uncle's shady connections had granted him insight into the slipshod security firm guarding the place. It was an organisation with more holes than a sieve, a fact Tom happily exploited.

Under the cloak of night, the trio rendezvoused half a mile from their target at the stroke of eleven. Black-clad and gloved, they slipped through these back streets like phantoms. Their attire was a blend of stealth and practicality, an ensemble designed to keep them hidden from prying eyes and forensics.

"These guys made a rookie mistake, leaving a single weak point outside," Tom remarked, his youthful demeanour belying his criminal know-how. "Shorting one of their panels will cascade down the line, rendering subsequent panels ineffective. We have to steer clear of those operational areas, though. We'll be ghosts until security arrives, which, by my calculations, should be around thirty minutes after we kick off."

"Nobody's playing games, right?" Marie's voice carried a stern edge.

"Oui, Mademoiselle," both her boyish comrades chimed in.

With synchronised watches and each one knowing their role, Tom axed through a plastic conduit to expose wires that entered the panel. With a bit of wiring trickery, he overloaded the panel's circuitry.

Nearby, bolt cutters made quick work of a stubborn padlock. The door yielded, they slipped inside, and sealed the entrance behind them.

Tom's sourced architectural blueprints directed them with a single purpose: to reach the manager's office. And there it was, inscribed with his name, Paul Jackson. After momentary resistance, Tom's dexterity got them in.

Marie took charge. "Try every drawer of the filing cabinet. We are looking for locked drawers only that contain hidden secrets. Our friend here, Locksmith Louie, can unlock them for us. Oui?"

Three pried open locked drawers revealed a trove of documents. The clock was ticking, forcing them to scan with urgency, seeking a connection between James Andersen's murder and the contents before them.

"Got something!" John's voice resonated with a mix of triumph and alarm. "A folder named James Andersen. Check this out! It's an inventory of firearms."

Marie came over to look. "See here? These are sales and they're all dated."

"Naughty. Naughty, Jimmy. Why were you buying illegal guns?" John remarked.

"Let's get outta here. Time's up!" Urgency in Tom's voice jolted the others to move.

Once downstairs, the outside door shot open and one, two, three they ran out into the night, following the predetermined route to avoid security. The mess left behind let the owners know what they had discovered.

On the drive back, reality hit. "Brian's innocence is just a fraction of this puzzle now," John conceded. "We've stumbled into the realm of organised crime, gun trafficking."

"Maybe," Marie said, "but that's not the reason for Andersen's demise. He must have needed those guns either to protect himself because of some nefarious activities he was involved in or to perpetrate some serious crimes."

United in their resolve, they trod a path fraught with danger, but their thirst for justice would not waver. They agreed to continue this perilous journey, despite being unsure they had the fortitude, or skill-set, to find all the answers.

Tom wanted to know, "So what do we do now?"

"Sleep on it." Marie said. "We won't be making any decisions tonight."

The decision to meet at noon later that day meant each of them went home to get some sleep.

Lunchtime arrived way too slowly for John and Tom, who were knocking at Marie's door right on time, hungry and ready to devour whatever she'd prepared. As the door opened, the aroma of crepes revved up their mood for food. Neither had ever eaten crepes before and the flavours of the fillings rocketed their taste buds to heaven's door, ranging from creamy garlic and mushroom to chocolate hazelnut with vanilla ice cream.

"Red or white for you, John?" Marie appeared with two bottles of wine.

"Water is fine for me, thanks, Marie. I haven't drunk alcohol since my seventeenth birthday."

"Red or white is fine with me, thanks," Tom butted in.

"Oh, ok." Tom was poured a less than generous serving of Merlot.

After eating, Marie sat back and watched the guys clean up the kitchen, before gathering them together.

Tom had an idea. "I was looking at other paperwork while you scanned Andersen's dealings. Those warehouse guys also have lists which show everything from the make, model and VIN to the new colour, mods and resale value of all the cars they stole."

"Interesting." John interjected. "Do you think Andersen is, I mean was, in cahoots with them and that's why they sold him the guns?"

The conversation went round in circles as they tried to come up with reasons this hypothesis might lead to his murder.

However, after a while, no closer to finding an answer, they fell upon a stroke of pure luck.

Marie and John took a leisurely stroll through the town centre, leaving Tom to watch TV. Thoughts and theories filled their conversation, but turned when Marie noticed an unusual pattern in the cars parked outside the Andersen dealership.

"Hey, that's odd. Some of those license plates seem too similar to be coincidental. The sequence of numbers keeps repeating." Intrigued, John approached to peer in through the dealership's window.

As he peered inside, his eyes widened in astonishment. The cars on display bore the same recurring license plate numbers. No one else seemed to have noticed the duplication.

"Why would they duplicate number plates, though?"

"The criminal fraternity uses car cloning or the illegal reproduction of license plates for theft, smuggling, or other illicit operations," Marie said. "It prevents authorities from finding the perpetrators of a crime when a car is used or fraudulently sold. And looking at the volume of cars with those plates, I'd say this is no small enterprise, and this business is knee deep in grand theft auto."

Without thinking, John said, "Isn't that a game?"

"This is no game!" Marie did not take kindly to John's nonchalance. "We are talking grand larceny, monsieur! We can also be sure his part in this enterprise led to his murder. Something took place that someone did not like."

"Or didn't take place," John chimed in.

At that moment, they saw a car pull out of the yard, being driven by Jane Harding. The opportunity to follow her and see if it led to them discovering something new was too good to miss.

Marie was unsure of the wisdom of this latest move. "I wish I knew whether we are wasting our time following her."

John had an idea and waited until reaching their destination before implementing it.

Jane pulled into the warehouse parking lot and made her way inside through large roller doors, which came down behind her to hide the hive of activity inside.

John and Marie pulled up over the road beside a wooded area.

"Did you see what was going on inside there?" It amazed John to see Jane at this warehouse.

Marie was keen to follow. "We should get a closer look."

"OK, but first let me pee behind that tree." John disappeared from view. Once alone, he wanted to see how their 'closer look' would turn out. The time machine transported him fifteen minutes into the future, but at that same spot. There, he watched as they entered the warehouse and waited to see what would happen.

A further fifteen minutes passed and the sound of gunfire came from inside the warehouse. John's blood ran cold. He hoped this didn't involve him and Marie.

After an hour's wait, they had not reappeared. It was now dark and several cars had left. There was no further activity.

John waited another hour, hoping like crazy that one or both would appear, but neither did. This answered Marie's question.

He returned the exact moment he'd left and appeared again from behind the tree.

"I don't think we should get any closer, Marie. We don't know what we'll find inside."

But Marie was adamant that they should proceed. A heated discussion ensued and John got into the car and threatened to drive away, at which point she agreed to leave with him.

Two blocks from home, a police car flashed them and told them to pull into a side alley. Neither was expecting the severity of the physical assault they were about to experience. An officer came to each side of the car and, without warning, pulled them both out before slamming them up against the hood. With guns pressed into the small of their backs, and their legs spread, a faux-search manhandled every body part through their clothing. However, as quickly as it all began, they stopped, returned to their car and drove away without a word.

John rushed around to Marie. "How you doin'?"

"I'll be OK. We are dealing with some seriously connected individuals, John. But I am not some weak and woolly woman that crap like this will intimidate. Come on!"

Back at the house, Tom had gone home, although the TV was still on. The enormity of what had happened hit them both, and Marie teared up. John stepped forward, his arms enfolding and drawing her into him. Marie's closeness, her perfume, and the sensitive desire in her eyes created an intense longing to kiss her.

He pulled back his head, and she pulled back hers. Both now peered deep into the other's eyes.

(Just a note from me. Not the narrator - the author. No kissy-kissy. Not in my book!)

John stopped. The pangs of morality he'd wrestled with during the past few days slapped him across the back of the head like a naughty boy. Now, in the stark reality of the moment, the truth became obvious. He had looked at Marie through the eyes of that teenage boy with a huge crush. His 2023 eyes, however, were more pragmatic. A romantic fling or relationship with an eighty-year-old would not be on the cards when he returned home, and his heart sank.

He backed away. "I'm sorry, Marie. No matter how I explain this, it won't make sense. I think I should apologise and leave."

John turned as Marie attempted to wrap her arm in his, but he slipped his arm away, stunning her with disappointment.

In a weakened voice Marie said, "Is that it? Are you giving up?"

"Yeah. We've tried, but there are forces greater than us at play here. It's over. We can guess, but we'll never be able to prove who killed him." He walked out, leaving a devastated Marie alone.

John's heart felt like it had gone through the wringer, so an errand at the sports book helped dull the pain. He entered with what he hoped would be a life-changing ticket, having been too busy to check the result. However, a pale-looking Jungo had checked and ushered him into a back room.

No one else went in and no sound came out. After ten minutes, though, a shriek of pain bellowed so loud that people half a block away came onto the street to investigate. A minute later, John walked out with a briefcase and the biggest, most arrogant grin from ear to ear.

He headed straight to the First National Bank in the middle of town. A new bank account received $100,000 and a safe deposit box deep in the vault got the remaining money. Back at the cashier, he signed an annual standing order that would pay for the box for years to come. He left the bank on Cloud Nine and wandered back to see Tom.

"We have tried everything to clear Brian's name. The three of us failed, so how much better will the two of us get on?" John asked his young friend.

"True." Tom rubbed his chin as he looked out the window. "You could go back to before the murder, though, hide inside the house, and see who killed him."

"Ooh! Woah! I'm in my fifties man. I'm no spring onion like you! And hiding has never been a forte of mine, either. Remember when you told me to hide in the bushes during our last ever math class so

Mr. Smooth, that physics teacher, wouldn't see us sneaking out? As he walked past, I stifled a sneeze, and he crapped himself. I got in so much trouble while you stayed hidden in the bush, and no one realised you were there."

Tom said, "I don't remember that. When was that?"

"Ah, true." John chuckled at his temporal confusion. "It hasn't happened yet. When it happens, though, you'll laugh so hard your cheeks will ache. Think I must have time travel lag. So much worse than jet lag, but without the deep vein thrombosis. Oh, I was just farting around. Go on then. I'll do it."

They set the watch to ten minutes before Tom had arrived for his burglary and aimed for the ballroom. With a shake of the device, John was gone.

"What's happening?" John had expected to just disappear and reappear as had occurred on each previous occasion he'd time travelled. Instead, he found himself barrelling down a psychedelic maze of tubes, completely cognisant of his travels. The tubes ended and freefalling in the dark, he waited for his life to end.

Wednesday 31st July 1986 7.01pm, Hometown

The sensation of transitioning from constant freefalling to standing on two feet at his destination, well, John's reaction spoke for itself.

"What the…?" With rapid breathing and heart racing, the surprise to still be alive and not splattered on rocks or a pavement, blew John away. With gratitude, he knelt and then lay prostrate on the ground, kissing it several times, before pulling himself together.

He'd arrived close to the doorway in question. Still a touch queasy, he entered the hallway, searching for a potential hiding place. Doors to several rooms presented themselves as possibilities, but the one leading down to the basement most interested him. It was opposite the ballroom. "Perfect," he thought, and pulled the door nearly closed, before waiting in the darkness.

He heard the first footsteps a few minutes later, which was Tom sneaking around. Cars pulled up, and more footsteps made their way into the ballroom. He didn't think it would be long before the murderer arrived.

Arrive they did, but not as John expected. From the dark, dingy basement came the creaking of a door, followed by footsteps approaching from behind him. They ascended the stairs towards his hiding place. Panic set in; he had to get out.

Off came his shoes, and he cracked the door open before sprinting towards the end of the hallway. From his new hiding place, John watched a tall individual walk towards the ballroom. Something distracted them. They detoured towards a side table in the hallway, fumbled with a gun and bullets that were lying out in the open, holstered the gun they'd arrived with, and continued.

A short time later, a deafening gunshot shattered the silence, jolting John into a paralysing grip of fear. Every fibre of his being screamed for movement, but his limbs remained frozen, a prisoner to his terror. Time stretched out as he stood immobilised, the echoes of the gunshot reverberating through his mind.

Amidst the chaos, another shot rang out, followed by the frustrated growl of a man and the hushed whispers of an unseen presence. John's senses heightened to fever pitch, his heart thundering in his ears as he struggled to regain control.

With a herculean effort, he wrenched himself from his stupor, only to stumble sideways into a cupboard filled with fragile glass ornaments. The crash reverberated through the house in a symphony of chaos. He refused to glance back and fought the urge to flee, his mind racing with indecision. Should he brave a look inside the room, or retreat to the safety of the shadows? As a silhouetted figure emerged from the ballroom, John froze, willing himself to blend into the darkness. With eyes barely open, he watched as the figure vanished through the front door, oblivious to John's presence.

John retreated. "What the hell am I doing?" However, after a few minutes, the itch of curiosity drove him closer to the tableau of death. Again, as he approached the ballroom, another figure, which he decided must be Brian, turned off the remaining lights and disappeared into the night. With no one else around, John put his shoes back on and inched forwards into the room, a shadow navigating shadows.

An unforeseen obstacle sent him sprawling, and he fell upon something cold and lifeless. Flooded with horror, he flailed arms, legs and everything to regain his footing away from what he knew must be the dead man. However, the residue of death lingered and the odour of blood permeated his nostrils. Lost in the moment, John absent mindedly wiped his hands on the floor, before considering his mistake and rubbing them through his hair. Eager to get himself far from the macabre comedy of errors, he turned to leave.

Thankfully, the basement door remained ajar, which gave him an escape route. With torch in hand, he set the devices and gave one a shake. There was the familiar flash, and he was out of there.

"No way!" John hurtled down the same tubes as earlier, but, aware it would not be fatal, settled in for the ride.

Saturday 23rd June 2023, 10.30pm, Hometown

Back home in 2023, John stood in disbelief. "What have I done?" In front of the bathroom mirror, he looked at the mess of blood covering his hands, head, and clothing.

The wet bloodied clothes came peeling off, as he almost wretched at the stench of death still ingrained within the fibres. They needed to be burned. But for now, he chucked them in the washing machine.

A cold shower helped invigorate his mind. However, as he watched the crimson evidence swirling down the drain, he knew there was plenty more evidence putting him at the crime scene.

A quick Internet search found news of James Andersen's murder. Almost forty years later, the murderer was still at large. The case was open and there were two suspects; Brian Harding and one other described as having left "bloodied prints".

The story of Brian's 1986 disappearance now took on a more personal meaning, and this train wreck was yet another setback. The travel couldn't continue as he became disillusioned at having spent so much time elsewhere, only to find tragedy and injustice. John was ready to return to the 80s, although having enjoyed spending time with his old friend, failure to find the truth left a void. He yearned for his normal life, so knew his return would be to say goodbye.

Tuesday 5th August 1986, 6.08pm, Hometown

Tom was keen to learn about the trip. "Did you see who it was?"

"No," was all John said, as his head drooped. "And it's time for me to leave. I left my mark. My fingerprints are everywhere. I fell over the body and wiped my hands all over everything!"

"What did you do that for?"

"I don't know! Maybe it was male menopause or something. My mind seized up. I don't know! The facts are, it happened and if I stay here, I will become a suspect."

Tom's mind returned to witnessing the murder. "You didn't knock something over in the hallway, did you?"

"Er, yeah. That would be me as well. You heard that, did you?"

"Hear it? I thought a war had started! First a couple of gunshots, and then as I was escaping, I heard what sounded like the ceiling had collapsed." Tom stopped and gave John a strange glance. "But how did I hear that when you only just did that now?"

John walked over to Tom, laid his hands on Tom's shoulders, and slapped both his cheeks. "Stop asking all these questions. Who do you think I am? Einstein? I don't know!"

Tom accepted some things go left unresolved, and a sadness overcame him, as he sensed the time had arrived to say goodbye. He'd enjoyed John more as an older dude than as one his own age, especially as now there was a fractured relationship with the younger guy.

John handed Tom a briefcase, knowing that if life followed the same path as before, this would be their last farewell. "Get busy livin', dude!"

With his mind focussed on John leaving, Tom placed the briefcase on the floor. "Will you continue to travel through time?"

"Not for a while. I think I'll take a break. Although I do have one detour to make on my way home." John was not in the mood for a long goodbye and wanted to get going.

With a vice-like grip, he shook Tom's hand and looked him in the eyes as he put on his best German accent. "Hasta La Vista, Baby."

Before a sarcastic remark about old people could form in Tom's brain, John gave the device a shake…and he was gone.

* * *

Despite Joe's disappearance with a flash in the alley, unbeknown to John, his travels through temporal realms had interconnected with those of others. Their fates and paths intertwined on plenty of occasions; sometimes for the better, but sometimes not.

EIGHT

STEVE

Some men aspire to great wealth. Many have a plan that includes hard work and careful planning. Steve Harding received no such encouragement from his parents, from the day he was born in February 1950, nor did the rest of their offspring. Life was lived by the seat of your pants in the Harding household.

If you had money for lunch, you ate. If you didn't, you ate someone else's lunch.

"Here, take a dollar," was Mr Harding's love language to his kids when he won big and had passed out before drinking all the winnings the same night.

Steve often didn't have basic things like everyone else, perhaps a pencil at school or socks. He also wanted things, like a kid's bike, as in some other kid's bike. And he usually got what he sought with ease because of his size, which encouraged him to attempt similar feats time and time again. However, when caught, a police officer took him home after being spoken to by his social worker. Once there, he would suffer a beating; not for stealing, but for getting caught. It was the Harding's parental guidance in the ways of the world.

On the few occasions he raised an objection as to the merits of his punishment, the response was always the same. "Quiet boy! It doesn't matter what you want." Rather than experience his father's belt or his mother's backhand, he held his tongue.

Steve's solace amidst the mayhem of family life was Ken, his older brother. "Mr Potato Head's weenie is teeny," was Ken's go to for helping Steve to smile and alleviate some of the pain, as well as a supportive arm around the shoulder and time spent talking. On occasions, he inadvertently called Ken dad, a word he rarely used for his own father.

One of Steve's wants took place on a hot and sticky afternoon in the summer of 1965. His thirst needed quenching whilst wandering down Main Street, and with little cash, he knew what to do. The wallet of a young man walking in front was hanging out of his back pocket. This was to be an easy opportunity to relieve him of more than just loose change.

Steve made his move, reaching out and snatching the wallet from the unsuspecting passer-by. There was the usual sense of satisfaction as he tucked it into his pocket and continued walking.

His moment of triumph was short-lived, however, as the same passer-by knocked into him, apologised, before helping him regain his balance; all the while deftly slipping the wallet from Steve's pocket.

It wasn't until a few minutes later that Steve realised the wallet was missing. He knew in an instant who had taken it and became angry and frustrated.

Now, Phil had been a pickpocket for years, and it had become second nature for him to be on a date or out at a party, and end up with four wallets by night's-end. He had set out that day to do a reverse con on whoever took the bait.

Little did Steve know, but Phil was watching from a distance, amused at his rage, and he couldn't resist the urge to rub it in his face. As he walked past Steve, the wallet dangled from his pocket once more. But it was the smirk that irked Steve the most. His instincts led him to take a swing at Phil, who evaded it with ease. "Nice try, tough guy."

Steve was livid, lunging at Phil again, fists clenched and trying to fight.

Phil laughed it off, amused by the bully-boy act. "Relax, man. You did a pretty good job with the wallet, but I can teach you a few things, if you're interested."

Steve calmed down, embarrassed at being outsmarted and admitted defeat. "Alright, you got me. You're a crafty son of a bitch."

"Yeah, I know." Phil smirked. "But, hey, maybe we can use our skills for something a lot more productive than just a few hundred bucks?"

Steve hesitated for a moment, then nodded. "OK, I'm listening. Let's grab a drink. You're paying."

A shared love of mischief, and the desire to make more money, bonded the two petty thieves from that day forward. Steve's toughness and opportunism blended well with Phil's tenacity and wit. They made a living, but it was nothing to boast about in the cells when they found themselves held on suspicion. (They always got off without conviction).

Phil and Steve became inseparable; a bond which was only to strengthen one wild, wet, and wintry day.

Steve had a habit of choosing the worst possible days to complete outdoor tasks. On this day, it was to pick up a second-hand bed using Phil's car because it was long enough to fit on the roof. All was fine until they carried the bed outside to the car.

"Where's the rope?" Phil inquired of his friend.

Steve shrugged. "Huh?"

Phil stopped walking and placed the uncovered bed on the snow-swept path. "How about the cover? Is that in the car?"

"Not unless you brought one." Steve also lowered his side to the ground.

Phil shook his head. "This is going to be fun," he said; his eyes looking to the sky, from which the white stuff now fell at a steady rate. "You sit in the back and hold one corner out the window. I'll tie a piece of string here and use that to hold the opposite corner whilst driving."

Two minutes into the escapade, Steve could no longer feel his hand. A minute later, as Phil turned right on red, having sped up to beat a car slowly making its way through the snow, the bed frame slipped off onto the middle of the crossroads and smashed into three pieces.

"Oh, shit!" Steve brought his hand inside, rubbing it to get the feeling back. "Don't stop."

Phil ignored the suggestion and pulled over to the kerb. Both got out, and between traffic lights, ran into the centre of the intersection to collect each of the large pieces. Steve was now able to sit in the front passenger seat, as the 3-piece bed fit inside the back of the car.

"What do you want to do with your new bed?"

"Could take it back and ask for a refund?"

Phil was agreeable to that, as he wouldn't be the one doing the asking. "OK," he said.

Steve burst into laughter. "No, let's just dump it somewhere and I'll sleep on the floor until I find something more robust than this piece of junk."

So, between them, they found a wooded area and dropped off the remnants of the bed, before retiring to Steve's place to relay the story to Ken.

Phil followed Steve around to the back door and felt a weird vibe as he watched his friend enter the house. Steve shouted, "Ken, you have to hear this!" Several people, unknown to Phil, were in the room, but no one said a word. Steve became quiet, studying their faces and wondering why they looked so sad.

Mr Harding appeared. "Ken's dead." His words and deeply furrowed brow combined with blood-shot eyes shot a shudder down Steve's spine, and his legs gave out from under him. Stunned silence filled the room before Steve asked, "How?"

"Got hit by a car on his motorbike," his father replied.

Steve looked at Phil, and without a word, walked out, followed by his friend. "Just drive," he said as they reached the car.

That long drive to nowhere gave Steve time to release his grief, and Phil was there to support him, just as Ken had always been until that point in his life. Somehow, in Steve's mind, that mantle now passed to Phil, who became his pseudo-anchor.

The area they differed the most was in their taste in women. Phil preferred long leggy blondes, while Steve had a thing for someone with a bit of meat on her bones. Neither could understand the other's preference, but at least it stopped them flirting with the same girl on a Saturday night.

Steve followed Phil's lead on how to progress their dishonest enterprise, however. Simple pick-pocketing got them by, but it was burglaries that stepped them up to a more satisfactory income bracket. The plan was to rob a couple of residences on most weekends, but never in the same town within a six-month period. They were more opportunists than planners, although that changed over the years, as their crime wave was countered by neighbourhood watches and public education.

They matured to robbing high-end homes, and one house topped their list, which was right in Hometown. Its grandeur and rooms, that reportedly flowed with antiques and art, made it a mouth-watering proposition for an upcoming burglar finding his way in the world. Phil calculated that a modest haul would garner them each at least $100,000.

They believed a month-long stakeout would provide insight into the activities, allowing them to remain undetected.

Friday 4th July 1975, 11:59pm, Hometown

Phil figured the 4th of July holiday to be the ideal opportunity to take on his biggest ever heist. People occupied themselves with celebrations, fireworks, and social gatherings on Independence Day. The likelihood of anyone noticing suspicious activity or being vigilant would be less than usual, and the festive atmosphere would serve as a distraction.

The day held symbolic significance representing freedom and independence, which appealed to Phil's rebellious nature and desire to live life on his own terms. A robbery on this particular day was Phil's way of reclaiming his own version of freedom, albeit through illicit means.

Steve was there for the ride, as Phil's heart was set on this being the pinnacle of his mediocre career.

Midnight struck, and both men made their way through the garden and up to the grand house, avoiding lights and taking great care with each step. The late hour provided the advantage that most revellers had succumbed to the drowsiness of their indulgences.

An unlocked window was the perfect opportunity to slip inside, their shadows disappearing into the darkness of the surrounding building. The sounds of music and faint murmurs seeped through the walls from the rear of the house.

"This party's in full swing." Phil knew that for them, though, it was just getting started.

Creaky floorboards reminded them to tread lightly. Each room held a trove of riches, illuminated by the soft glow of moonlight that flittered through the open curtains. Gilded frames adorned with masterpieces lined the walls, while exquisite chandeliers cast shimmering lights on the polished floors below.

They remained as far from the party as possible, pocketing fine silverware, golden antiques, and various oddities that seemed valuable. Each item added to the financial tally Steve kept in his head.

An inebriated guest came strolling towards them, trying to hug them both, but only Steve took up the offer. "What are you hiding in those bags, lads? She laughed before continuing her journey, oblivious to pretty much everything.

Time was not on their side and their backpacks had grown heavy.

In a dimly lit corridor, the two exchanged knowing glances, their eyes reflecting a mixture of triumph and nervous excitement. They had achieved what they'd come for. It was time to retreat into the night.

Steve slipped as he followed Phil out the window and made such a racket, with his bag hitting the ground outside, that a not-so-drunk guest raised the alarm. A posse formed within seconds, and the host appeared with a shotgun.

Phil had a head start, but Steve soon passed him. "Run!" he screamed.

Their narrow escape showed Steve he'd bitten off more than he'd bargained for. He needn't have worried, though. Life as he knew it was about to come to an abrupt end. Instead of getting to benefit from instant riches, on arriving home he found the watch and funny-looking device, which changed his life, as July 1975 disappeared with a flash of light.

Friday 7th March 1930, 7.03pm, Liverpool

Steve found himself in a narrow, cobble-stoned street. It was dark. It was raining and, being dressed for summer, he was instantly cold. The disorientation of time travel compounded the whole situation.

"What planet is this?" His eyes tried to find some semblance of normality.

Fearful and insecure, he clambered to his feet. Life's school of hard knocks taught him to handle tough times, but one of his toughest classes was about to start.

Warmth and dry clothes were his first priorities and his life of crime and pushing others around helped get what he wanted.

He grabbed the first solo man he came across into an alley way and provided an ultimatum. The accosted person could give him his coat, trousers, shirt, shoes and socks or experience a beating, after which he'd take them, anyway.

At that moment, Steve heard the familiar Irish lilt he knew from home.

"Will yer be havin' me cap and me underwear too, while yer at it?" came the unexpected response.

Steve was stunned into silence and all anger fell away, as the beauty of that accent he loved so well tamed him like a cat.

"Sorry, man! Let me buy you a drink." Not that he had money nor any idea where the pubs were.

"Listen, I t'ink I should buy you a drink. You look positively under-dressed and could catch your death any minute. Your clothing is so threadbare. Do you not have money for anything more?"

The bemused traveller followed his companion to a pub at the end of the road where there was a hearth with a fire. Inside was like heaven.

"Where am I?" Steve asked, hoping to get some idea of what had happened.

"You're in The Belvedere." The forty-something gentleman shook the rain from his coat. "Now, what'll you have?"

"A Bud or a Heine." Steve stood by the fire, warming every body part. "Yeah, but where are we? What's the name of this town?"

"What's a Bud or a Heine? Where are you from? You're not from Liverpool, to be sure." They both gave each other a strange look.

"Liverpool! England! How did I get here?" Steve's voice went up an octave and twenty decibels.

The middle-aged Irishman offered a hand to shake and introduced himself as Hamish. "I have no idea, young man, But I'll buy you a beer, anyway." And he headed off to the bar.

"Quaint bar. Very authentic. And I love how everyone is in fancy dress. Is it just tonight you all wear your grandparents' hand-me-downs, or is it always like this?" Steve began to dig himself a hole.

"Hey! You wanna fight?" A rough-looking guy in the corner stood, wobbled over and stood face to face with him.

"Well, I wasn't, but I could make an exception." With water still dripping off his clothes, Steve turned to approach the potential assailant, happy to take on the challenge.

"Handbags ladies." Hamish returned with the drinks and diffused the tension. The drunk in the corner laughed, while Steve looked around for which handbags and ladies he was referring to.

"Is this a themed bar?" Steve looked bemused. "That guy is reading a newspaper from 1930."

Hamish now looked bemused. "That's today's paper. What's the craic with that?"

"What? Today is 1930?" Steve scoffed. "Prove it."

Hamish took Steve by the hand, thinking he must be delusional from the cold, and found a warm coat and some shoes for him to borrow, and offered a bed at his place. They walked the short distance to Hamish's humble tenement building, where Steve's exhaustion meant he quickly nodded off to sleep.

The morning light and voices in the room awoke the now dried off traveller. Steve arose to receive a warm greeting from his hosts. The view from the fifth-floor window of the building made him realise he probably was in 1930 Liverpool. There could be no other explanation as he saw the soot on the buildings, so many cobbled roads, and impoverished people. This was not Hometown circa 1975.

He wondered what got him there, or whether he was crazy. This would mean he had time travelled, but that was impossible. His mind churned to figure out what was possible.

One thing about Steve, though, he loved adventure, which usually involved stealing things and/or punching someone. What a treat it would be to find what 1930s Liverpool offered a young, fit man in his twenties.

Hamish had been helpful and kind, but he was not the sort of person to direct Steve towards the action he desired. So, after experiencing a communal bathroom and true Irish hospitality, he dressed for the conditions and walked off to see who and what fun the city offered.

Once outside, Steve's mind whirled as he wandered down one street and then the next. The air had a smoke-like taste, and he gazed at everything and everyone; bumping into people on purpose to create conversations that helped immerse him in his surroundings.

After an hour, he came across parkland. A gentle stroll through Newsham Park was like stepping into a serene oasis away from the hustle and bustle. Tall, majestic trees lined the pathways and, being a Saturday, lots of families were out and about. Steve was determined to talk with some of them and learn about life.

Unimpressed at how dowdy men dressed and that women all had long skirts and wore hats, he decided not to take any clothing home as a souvenir.

The central jewel of the main boulevard was a fountain encircled by the figures of four white horses. Della Rabbia Fountain was the perfect place to engage with passers-by.

An attractive young woman with beautiful long red hair and blue eyes made Steve's jaw drop as she stopped to admire the attraction. Without hesitation, he approached her and tried to impress. "Italian sculpted with only the best marble. I'd say 1800s, maybe 1864." He had no clue what he was talking about.

She didn't know how to respond except to say, "I think you mean limestone."

She looked up, as Steve became enamoured by her smile, and did his best to regain some self-respect. Despite often being gruff and tough, he could change in an instant, with the right motivation, to become considerate in ways that could charm the socks off a snake.

"You, er, already knew that, didn't you?" His leg swung to kick a stone, but missed and kicked the wall instead. "Aw, am I making a fool of myself? I'm Steve, by the way."

"Joyce Tuttle. Nice to meet you. Are you American?" Steve's awkwardness and foreign accent drew the young lady's eyes towards his as they shook hands.

He gestured and asked if she'd like to walk with him. The smell of newly cut grass and blooming flowers filled the air, while bird song blended with the rustling of leaves, creating a gentle symphony of nature. Their stroll passed a tranquil lake shimmering in the sunlight, which reflected the surrounding beauty, helping create the perfect ambience for Steve's intentions.

"Do you dance?" Joyce asked.

"I can boogie. If that's what you mean." Steve demonstrated his idea of a boogie. Joyce's jaw dropped at the sight of a man moving his hips in ways that seemed unnatural. Although she seemed to enjoy it.

"No. Not really. Never mind." She bowed her head, wishing she hadn't mentioned it.

Steve would not give up, though. "We could dance if you'd like. Not now, of course. But some other time."

Joyce mentioned a dance that evening that they could attend together. But now she had an appointment that she was already late for. They agreed to meet at The Grafton Ballroom around 7pm before she hurried off.

With a few hours to kill, he made his way to the local market on the West Derby Road. A pilfered apple here and some bread there, his petty thieving remained the same, no matter which end of the twentieth century he was in. There was no obvious way to find where the dance was or to keep track of time, but street smarts got him there on time and helped make friends on the way.

Steve walked and talked with a colourful tapestry of characters as he passed rows of terraced houses, their smoke-filled chimneys exhaling the heavy stench of coal. Each individual told remarkable stories that wove a rich history into the fabric of the city.

His entrance into the venue needed to look stylish, to improve on the average first impression he'd made on Joyce earlier. As he weaved through a crowd, a master of deception amid chaos, Steve's fingers moved with practiced precision, deftly pilfering wallets from unsuspecting victims. Each stolen item was a small victory, a step towards his goal of blending into this unfamiliar world.

Determined to catch the eye, Steve sought a clothing shop and, hence, a shopkeeper, whose keen eye for fashion promised to transform him into a vision of sophistication. The careful selection of each garment and meticulous tailoring helped Steve shed his old identity like a snake shedding its skin. In its place emerged a new persona, one of elegance and refinement. The tailored suit clung to his frame, the fabric whispering secrets of wealth and privilege.

As he stepped out into the bustling streets, a surge of confidence swelled within. Every stride exuded an air of self-assurance, of a man reborn in the fires of reinvention. The sights and sounds had changed because the sun had set twenty minutes earlier. Busy intersections, trams rumbling by with their bells clanging and flickering gas streetlights casting an amber glow, gave Steve a thrill at experiencing what seemed unique.

He arrived at the entertainment centre of town, where people queued to enter the Grafton Ballroom. Steve was ready to make a grand entrance. He pushed open the double doors and stepped inside. A smoky haze hung in the air as couples glided across the polished dance floor. The lively sounds of jazz filled the room, punctuated by laughter and clinking glasses. The Ballroom was alive with energy and brimming with anticipation.

Heads turned and his presence silenced some conversations, as Steve moved with charisma and a swagger that commanded attention. At least that's what he told himself. In reality, one woman on her own at the back of the room noticed him and made a beeline straight for him. Her buxom body was on course to manhandle him had someone more preferable not intervened.

"Hello, handsome," came a familiar voice. "So happy to see you again. Ready to dance?" Joyce placed her arm in his and nuzzled in. Once on the dance floor, their bodies didn't move in perfect harmony or glide with any sort of rhythm, but Steve picked up moves and improved as the evening progressed. They enjoyed his learning process, along with a few laughs and trodden on toes.

It wasn't so much their bodies that found their rhythm as their eyes. The depth of Joyce's gaze captivated Steve with an allure he could not resist. As their dancing improved, every twirl and spin deepened their connection. They exchanged unspoken desires and secret yearnings through a growing chemistry. Steve considered Joyce to have a seductive power that danced with mischief, and having been mischievous his whole life, now was not the time to resist.

Neither of them was ready for what came next, allowing impulses to take control, as sensuality overcame common sense. A secluded side room away from prying eyes and ears provided the opportunity they sought. They were quick. They were full of passion. And they were surprised at how five minutes of carnal lust could be so exhausting. The slow, casual stroll back into the ballroom, through the crowd and out into the night hid the reality of their liaison.

Both enjoyed their time together, in the park and throughout the evening, but knew it was best to call it a night.

"Let's go dancing again some time." Joyce looked hopeful that they would see each other again.

Steve was already unsure if he had done the right thing, but would not let on. "Sure, that would be cool."

He walked her to a taxi, kissed her goodbye, and paid the driver to take her home.

Steve was a charmer, but not one for a relationship. He had been in similar circumstances before, but never in this unusual a situation. It made him uneasy. Wandering the cobbled streets down to the river, he decided it would be a good idea to leave, but what did he need to do to travel through time and space again?

He sat on the wharf beside the River Mersey and brought out the two items that were still with him from 1975. Steve attempted to figure out how they worked. The watch must set the destination time, and the gadget the location, but what the gadget's numbers meant was beyond him. To leave Liverpool, those numbers had to change. But where would they take him next?

"Set them both and get outta here," he thought. But also, when to go to? "The future must be some kind of wonderful. I'd love to experience one hundred years into the future."

Steve was uneducated, so unaware that randomly setting the location had a high probability of ending up in the ocean. Although they had been stuck previously, he now spun the knobs with little resistance, and when they stopped, the two sets of four dials read 34,00,32,N and 118,29,45,W. After setting the watch, he was ready to go.

At that moment, he noticed three men coming towards him at pace. Stylish clothes worn by an isolated individual were a classic target for a mugging. He knew what they were after and needed to get out of there now.

There was one problem. How to activate the time machine? Steve racked his brain to remember what he was doing when he left 1975, but now, surrounded by thugs spouting threats, that seemed the least of his worries.

One came from behind and grabbed his arms in a full nelson. Another right up into his face, screaming as spit flew into his face and mouth. As the screamer's first punch came at him, Steve had a premonition and shouted, "Shake it!" With the device in his right hand, that's precisely what he did.

NINE

CALIFORNIA TIME

Alfie had a three-day pass from his duties as a private in the army. He hoped to spend the time with his mother at home in Liverpool. However, Edith heard he was available and made sure she was the first one to grab him to come out with her. In two minds, he agreed, and they walked for a while. She wanted more than a walk, though, and soon enough she embraced him passionately and puckered up, ready to kiss him. Alfie wasn't sure whether to be pleased or disappointed when, in the nick of time, two friends he hadn't seen for a year came running round the corner; a publican chasing close behind, wanting payment for the beer they'd stolen.

The leader recognised Alfie and slowed to a jog. "Hey, Alfie! Haven't seen you in ages, mate. Great to see you. Come and have some fun." Without waiting, he ran off.

Alfie, being both a bit of a ladies' man and a man's man, although in two very different ways, became torn between the options...for three seconds. He looked at Edith and back at the guy, whose name he couldn't remember, then back at Edith. "Sorry babe! Gotta go," he said, as he wriggled free before joining the footrace.

The publican's pursuit lasted another few seconds, but the bunch of them were gone and heading for the riverside.

After several bottles of booze, the boisterous group noticed a stylish well-dressed man down by the water. "I bet he has a few bob," the leader said. "Come on, let's go have a chat."

As they approached, the stranger looked to be trying to do something. "Grab him from behind," the ringleader said, at which Alfie put him in a full nelson. Now up in his face, the main perpetrator made clear what they wanted. "Give us all your money, or Alfie here will break your arms." With no response, he provided some encouragement, throwing a punch straight at the guy's nose. However, before his fist could reach its mark, there was a flash of light and the victim was gone.

* * *

Friday 5th July 2075, 7am, Santa Monica

Steve's 1930s chic did not look so cool in 2075, especially when you are standing in the Pacific Ocean with water up to your waist. He had landed beside Santa Monica Pier, and like the previous journey, was instantly soaking wet, fifty metres from barriers that protected the elevated walkway from the sea. Fifty metres further out to sea and he would have struggled to survive.

A more pressing and obvious issue needed to be dealt with, however. Alfie still had hold of him.

"What The F...!" Alfie's grip loosened as Steve knew what was happening, but his adversary did not. The sudden disorientation enabled Steve to force himself free, turn and, before Alfie could complete his expletive, slam him with a left hook. Blood spurted from the nose as the head rocked backwards. Aware that the device was in his right hand, and desperate not to break it, Steve followed with a knee to the groin, which brought Alfie to his knees, before rushing up to shore.

The bloodied ruffian staggered to his feet. With hands cupped over his genitals, fury blazed in his eyes as he lunged forward. "Come here, you bastard!" His pursuit, fuelled by pure adrenaline, brought him towards dry land, splashing in frantic anger. When he emerged from the water, his target was already far ahead.

Steve knew he had to use every trick in the book to outwit his relentless foe. He started by discarding everything on top but his ruffled shirt and joined the early morning joggers heading towards Venice Beach. Passers-by paused, their curiosity piqued by the sight of two men dressed like relics, pounding along Ocean Front Walk in clumpy old shoes. It looked like some sort of avant-garde reality program was being filmed, while others watched in astonishment as the gap between pursuer and pursued narrowed.

Steve remained focused; his determination unwavering as he pushed himself forward, planning to reach Venice Beach first, and somehow evade this thug in the labyrinth of side streets.

The trailing pursuant had time to consider his surreal predicament, whilst running through surroundings that must have seemed more alien than foreign. He must have wished he'd ignored Edith's persistence to go for a walk. But right at that moment, mad as hell, he focussed on battering the guy ahead before finding out what was happening. The temperature was already so much hotter than Liverpool and his pace was slowing, but army training and adrenaline gave him the impetus to press on.

Steve tired, his chest burning, not being used to so much exercise. Blisters hurt both heels, caused by such uncomfortable shoes. Venice Beach was getting closer and there were already a fair number of people milling around. A quick look back brought a shock to the system. Alfie was so close.

Laughter and crashing waves at Venice Beach offered no solace against the inevitable looming attack. Alfie's anger boiled over. With each stride, his fury intensified, driving him forward, until, as he was about to nab his target, he tripped. A sudden burst of energy lunged him forward, his hand outstretched, grabbing hold of Steve's shirt and wrangling him to the ground. "Got you, you little bastard!" The triumph and relief were clear in his voice. Their paths converged in one heart-stopping moment, as both flailed on the concrete, trying to land a blow. Alfie's fingers closed around Steve's shoulder before he spun his adversary around.

A crowd of onlookers surged forward, seeing one man about to unleash his vengeance on the other; their voices raised in protest. Joggers and beachgoers alike united to detangle the wretched bodies. Surprised by the unexpected intervention, Alfie hesitated, his grip faltering as the weight of the crowd pressed in around him. A human barrier formed between them; their collective presence serving as a bulwark against violence, frustrating Alfie.

Steve sensed an opportunity to slip free, his breath coming in ragged gasps as he retreated to safety amidst the throng. Hence, he took full advantage and disappeared into a mix of side streets and gardens, making it impossible for Alfie to find him.

For Alfie, the taste of bitter defeat lingered. Yet the futility of his quest for vengeance must have dawned on him, as he found himself in a world not his own.

Steve was now alone and able to consider his new environment. A change of clothes was his primary concern. The shops were closed, so stealing some cash was the way to go. His present attire would not make it easy to go unnoticed, which meant instead of the usual subtlety of pick-pocketing, brute force would be required.

A mark was soon identified. He ensured they weren't Irish, and pulled them into a quiet alley to scare them into handing over their wallet. Except he chose the wrong mark. The rough scare tactics only made the guy angry, and his taekwondo left Steve flat on his back after a quick punch to the chest and swiping his legs. So far, the twenty-first century wasn't the utopia he'd dreamed of.

As a result, he adopted a new strategy to wait and watch how the world worked before making any further rash decisions.

When the shops opened, trying to figure out how people paid for things was bewildering. Curiosity led him to enter a quirky clothing store. A riot of bright tie-dye garments hung on racks, while the scent of joss sticks hung in the air, invoking a sense of 1970s déjà vu. The lack of cash registers and curious nonchalance of both customers and staff puzzled Steve. Customers picked what they liked and sauntered out of the shop without a transaction or a protest.

He observed for a while, mesmerised by the spectacle, before a young lady approached to ask if she could help.

"Can I have one of those in a forty-inch chest?" He picked out a greenish tie-dye top.

She handed him the shirt, and Steve asked for a fitting room.

"You can use the mirror if you'd like," she said.

He got snappy. "I want to see how it fits and how it looks on me."

"Come here." She beckoned him over and placed the shirt against his body, gesturing towards the mirror. Dumbfounded, he saw himself don the shirt in the reflection. He raised his arms, and the image seamlessly followed his movements. "Interested in seeing yourself in pink?"

"Yeah, sure," he agreed, all scepticism melting away. The mirror cycled through seven different colour options. Steve was smitten.

"I'll take it in green, plus a pair of those shades."

"They aren't shades. They're night glasses."

"Night vision, you mean?" Steve had read about night vision goggles being used during the Vietnam conflict.

"Ha! No," she replied with a touch of disbelief. "Never heard of night glasses? You wear them at night and it looks like daytime."

"Yeah?" Steve's eyes widened with excitement. "I'm having those!"

He surveyed the area for any additional high-tech gadgets. "What are Air ASICS?"

"Now, that is a new range. It is not exactly a gym shoe or a running shoe. It's more of a flying shoe," she said, removing one from behind the protective shield. "You literally walk on air."

Without pausing, he tried on a size seven pair and bounced around the shop, a few inches off the ground.

He had one final question. "What are they using those changing rooms for when they have no clothes?"

At the far end of the shop, a row of what looked like changing rooms had people coming and going, but no one carried clothes to try.

"That is our latest nanotech range. There's a room free. Try it out and see what suits you."

Steve entered a room full of unbelievable technology. For the next hour, he described his ideal garments to a multi coloured screen on the wall, and a robotic arm crafted them onto his body. The lightness of the attire made it akin to a second skin. The descriptions coming from the chatty screen claimed the garments to be waterproof, temperature-regulating along with health-monitoring wonders and other fantastical feats. Steve found the experience both awesome and unnerving.

With the shirt, shoes and glasses in hand, he proceeded to the exit, like everyone else. However, an invisible barrier at the doorway bounced him back. His second attempt was just as futile. He was stuck inside.

The shop assistant came over to help. "Do you have enough credit?"

"Enough credit? I don't know."

"If the credits in your account haven't automatically paid for the goods, the barrier won't let you out," she said.

Steve looked stupefied before enquiring as to the cost. The total came to $6,750, so he returned all the items and walked through the doorway a free man.

He realised that to stick around for a few days, he'd need credit to at least buy food.

Overhead, whirring sounds drew his attention to small, unmanned helicopter-like things which flew in all directions. "What's that all about?" he asked passers-by. No one answered. They were all too busy dancing, singing, or talking in their own little world.

Further attempts to attain a response got nowhere. His right hand clenched into a fist and his eyes searched furtively for a victim. About to pounce, a peculiar scene unfolded above him. From nowhere, a gargantuan automobile emerged from a window on the first floor of a building bearing the name Tesla. It dangled precariously in mid-air, extending about fifteen metres beyond the building's edge. The contraption pirouetted gracefully, revealing every intricate detail of its underbelly before retreating into the building and vanishing from view.

Steve froze, lost in a world of sensory overload. An irresistible curiosity gnawed at him, melting all angst, and urging him toward this enigmatic Tesla establishment.

He strolled inside to find a bright white car showroom. A tall man in his early fifties approached wearing a shirt with a big black X on it.

"Hi there. You must be new around here. How can I help?

"Show me your fastest car." Steve was so excited, wanting more astounding feats.

"I'm Elon, the nano-manager here at Tesla. Of course, no trouble at all." Steve was in awe of this personal attention from whatever a nano-manager was. "May I inquire as to your name?"

"Steve. Steve McQueen." He looked up at Elon with a smirk and eased himself into the driver's side. "Where does the driver sit?"

Elon's response was cryptic, yet intriguing. "The car is the driver, Steve. Relax and savour the journey."

Steve drove several vehicles within a convincing and immersive simulation without leaving the building. After such a mesmerising experience, he went to shake hands.

"You're a hologram! This is way too cool!" He looked around to see that an array of Elons were presenting cars to potential customers throughout the showroom. With a contented grin on his face, Steve took his leave, exiting another surreal twenty-first century experience.

He strolled through the shopping precinct. "What's next?"

There was now the hustle and bustle of a normal Friday in a busy town and his clothing no longer stood out as unusual. In fact, there didn't seem to be any particular style or fashion. Everyone seemed to be individualistic with their own style, which he slipped into with ease.

People talking while walking freaked him out, because it wasn't as if they were talking with someone. They were alone. Who were they talking to? Seemingly demented individuals engaged in one-sided conversations. Had human nature become even more self-absorbed? This didn't seem right. Were psychiatric wards so full that these people walked free? What had caused such widespread behaviour?

Curious, he grabbed someone. "Who are you talking to?"

"Hands off, weirdo! I'm on the phone to my mom," came the response.

The phone? Where did they hide the receiver? Some appeared to have hearing aids and others wore glasses, but where was the phone? With his mind boggled, he gave up on that quest.

The air was hotter than Steve was used to, making him parched rather than the simple 'I could do with a drink' kind of thirst. So, the time had arrived to do something he was good at, steal stuff he could exchange for cash.

Twenty minutes later, he came across some less affluent members of society. The sheer number of people queued at the food bank surprised him. "With all that tech, what has caused so many people to be impoverished?" he thought. "Something must have gone seriously wrong!" He considered joining the end of the line, but feared he might be so scrawny by the time he reached the front, it wouldn't be worth it.

Thirty minutes later, houses on the more affluent side of the scale came into view, which is what he'd been searching for.

Steve banked on human nature being the same in twenty-first century America as it was back in the 1970s. In his experience, a select few practiced home security and police rarely responded to burglaries with any urgency.

He caught sight of a house nestled on the street corner, a solitary sentinel separated from the world by a looming fence and an abundance of unruly shrubbery.

Whilst scanning for signs of life, he strolled up the winding driveway to the house, where he tested each window like a seasoned burglar, searching for an entry point. And there it was, his portal to the forbidden world within; an open first-floor window overlooking the secretive haven of the back garden. In no time at all, he was inside.

Steve knew speed was of the essence when robbing a house, and after only ten minutes was ready to leave with a bag full of small valuable items. Within seconds he was in the garden, and ran round to the front, where he stopped dead in his tracks. A group of vigilante neighbours were walking up the driveway with baseball bats, golf clubs and a gun. How did they know he was there?

Back around the house, he ran, clambering up and over a fence into a neighbouring garden. No one was there, so he ran through to the next. After scrambling over several fences and through numerous gardens, he hoped to have found safety, and walked out onto the road. He'd taken the opportunity to change clothes whilst rummaging through the house and now walked with a spring of confidence in his step.

Unfamiliar with Santa Monica, he headed south, hoping to find buyers for his loot back in Venice.

Discrete enquiries in a bar led to a sombre looking Italian called Dave. They made a deal and Steve now had $15,000 on some sort of gadget that his thumb activated. He ordered a beer and some chips. When the bill arrived, he realised $15,000 wouldn't buy as much as he'd hoped.

As Steve walked outside into the early evening rays, his relief at having money helped him relax and become more aware of his twenty-first century surroundings.

At the kerbside, waiting for the familiar green Walk sign, he noticed how organised all the vehicles seemed as they passed. The Walk sign appeared, but Steve stepped back and watched, fascinated by how everything stopped, as if on cue. Pedestrians behaved the same as in 1975, though, with stragglers reaching the opposite side well after the Don't Walk sign showed. A few seconds later, all the cars moved off together, accelerating in unison and, similar to the Teslas, they were driverless. The organised movement was like a well-choreographed dance, in stark contrast to the mayhem he knew back home.

Away from the kerb, he observed all the goings on around him with a sense of wonder. In amongst the pedestrians, individuals looked to be hailing cabs. They didn't choose a vehicle, but shouted "Shaxi!", and seconds later, an empty car would pull over beside them. With barely a hindrance to the flow of traffic, it removed itself from the pack of cars.

Steve watched multiple times, as on every occasion random people, who looked to be independent of the hailer, also got into the car before it drove away.

"I gotta have a go at that!" he told the old lady beside him, who had been with him the whole time he'd been watching everything. She wasn't taking in the atmosphere like Steve, however. She told him she'd forgotten where she was.

"Oh, that's lovely. Take me with you, Dear. You could take me home. I think I know where I live."

"Come on. Let's give this a go." They approached the kerb and Steve shouted out, "Shaxi!" while waving his arm.

Nothing happened for a few seconds, until, from nowhere, a large vehicle slid across two lanes through a parting in the waves of traffic, and pulled up right beside them in a lane void of moving vehicles.

"Oh my…" The side door opened slowly with a pneumatic whooshing sound. "So cool!" Steve stood, watching in amazement.

"Hurry up, Dear. Get in." Now they had a vehicle, the old lady became a touch impatient to get home.

He helped her inside and sat himself down, as five people appeared from nowhere and sat beside them. Without a clue what was happening, he waited for whatever came next. A female voice said, "Thank you for choosing Shaxi."

Steve's jaw dropped and his eyes turned dreamy. "Who was that?"

"Before we begin, please fasten your seatbelt."

"Who are you? And where are you?" Steve looked all around,

unable to find this hidden beauty.

"Fasten your belt, man." An unimpressed older gentleman with his cap on backwards gave Steve a dig. "You're holding us all up."

Steve clipped his belt in place.

"Thank you," the voice said, at which point Steve gave up his search for romance. The door closed, and into the traffic they glided.

"Your credits have all been recognised. Please state your destinations." One by one, each person gave an address, including Steve's elderly friend. Steve himself, however, had no idea where he wanted to go, so gave the vicinity of Pacific Palisades, which he'd seen on a billboard somewhere. Once all addresses were in, she announced, "First stop, 1823 Hill Street, Santa Monica."

Steve looked around at everyone and everything, and with great excitement blurted out, "What is this Shaxi thing?"

A middle-aged man in shorts, vest and flip-flops replied, "You're not from around here, are you? Where are you from?"

"You wouldn't believe me if I told you."

"You're not Welsh, are you?" came the response from a young lady wearing a baseball cap.

"Not that I'm aware of. No." The signs of a cheeky smirk showing on his face. "So, what is Shaxi?"

Everyone replied almost in unison, "Shared Taxi."

"Thought you knew. You're the one who hailed it," said the young lady. "All we did was take advantage of someone getting a Shaxi nearby.

"Don't you know each other?" Steve asked.

"Nah, man!" laughed a well-groomed African American lady. "I know him," prodding the young man beside her, "too well! He my beau. But I ain't never laid eyes on any of these before in my life."

"Shaxi must own a lot of these taxis. They must have an entire fleet of vehicles, hey?" Steve looked around. Who would answer next?

"No, Dear." His elderly friend patted him on the hand like he
was her grandson, and she pitied him for being a little dim. In a slow,
gentle voice, she said, "These are all private vehicles. While the
owners aren't using them, they get used as Shaxis to earn some pocket
money. Have I dumbed it down enough for you, Dear?"

Without hesitation, Steve replied, "Thank you, Granny."

Her eyes rolled back. "Smart ass!"

With continued interest, Steve asked, "But how do they know to
stop when there's no one in the car? And how do all those other cars
let them through the traffic so efficiently?"

The young lady leant across, her eyes fixed on Steve's. After an
almost eerie pause, she asked, "Are you sure you want to know?"

"Yeah. That's why I asked."

"Aliens," she replied. Everyone erupted into laughter, except for
Steve, who joined them after a brief pause, unsure if there was some
inside joke he was missing. "No. Just joshing with you. AI, man.
Artificial Intelligence. This is my field of study at USC. All those
vehicles are in constant communication with each other and with the
world around them. You shout Shaxi, and they come running."

A thrill of fantasy tingled Steve once more, as his invisible woman
announced, "1823 Hill Street, Santa Monica." The vehicle stopped and
the young lady exited. "Great talking with you. Bye."

The rest of Steve's shared journey included people leaving and
others entering along the way. Before his Pacific Palisades destination,
they arrived at the old lady's home. As he went to help her up and
out, she turned to him and, with a dead-pan face, said, "Go home and
don't come back." She grabbed his hand, and as she withdrew hers, a
folded piece of paper remained with Steve. Undeterred by her strange
behaviour, he returned to the car without a word. Once inside, the

unfurled paper revealed "1975". His shock turned to dread that the old lady was part of some sinister plot linked to his past.

After alighting the Shaxi, he booked into a hostel, bought a couple of burgers and more chips, and got a six-pack to calm his nerves and wash it all down. Out on the esplanade overlooking the sea, he struggled to relax. But with the grandeur of the Californian sunset everywhere he looked, his grandfather's favourite saying came to mind. "A man's fortune goes far beyond riches." Steve deemed himself fortunate indeed, as his worries dissolved in the moment's beauty.

Once the sun dropped below the horizon, he packed up his gear, returned to the hostel, and went to bed.

Tap. Tap. Tap. It wasn't a heavy touch on his shoulder, but enough to wake Steve, his eyes opening to notice the blurry outline of someone stood before him.

"Listen. Don't talk. Go back to 1975 and stay there!"

With that, they walked away, leaving Steve alone.

"What the heck was that all about?" He rolled over, his eyes closed and heart racing, worried that he wouldn't get back to sleep. He didn't. Thought after worrying thought reverberated through his mind, rehashing those same words, whilst considering whether they were linked to the old lady.

Sleep came as dawn broke, but he woke up half an hour later as a tall, bald guy belched into his left ear, having returned from a satisfying breakfast.

Too tired to care, Steve looked at him through bleary eyes and muttered, "Could've been worse, man. Could've been the other end."

Now he was awake once more. "Should I go home or enjoy a vacation?" Life in 2075 seemed so complicated, and for a moment Steve wished he was back in "good old 1975". Such a quandary, but considering he may not get this opportunity again, he stayed.

With credits in hand, the first thing to do was to stock up on the items he'd handed back the previous day. After a less eventful Shaxi ride to Santa Monica, he walked out of the shop barrier-free, acting like some bigshot with heaps of fantastic toys.

The experience of such unfamiliar streets created a sense of adventure and the desire to explore. However, that changed when he noticed someone unnerving coming his way. He needed a second look to be sure, as the individual's attire differed from how Steve remembered. It was the scouse thug from 1930 and he was shouting something.

He knew the guy was bigger, fitter, and faster than him, so Steve turned and tried to flee, but it was too late. The large arm of the lout grabbed his shoulder. Steve relaxed, awaiting the inevitable.

"Hey you!" Alfie grabbed Steve's hand and shook it. "I don't know how to thank you. This place is incredible. I love it! No more army, beautiful warm weather, gadgets galore, and the girls love me. Something about my accent, I think. And look! They even fixed my nose."

"Ah, cool. You're enjoying yourself, then?" Steve retrieved his hand from Alfie's vice-like grip. "Do you want to go back now?"

"No way! I'm staying! You know, like, I saw you in the distance and wanted to say there are no hard feelings. No idea how we got here, but who cares when life is this great, hey?" And with that he was off, hooking up with a carload of girls that stopped to whisk him away.

Steve stood in stunned silence, jealous that he didn't have Alfie's remarkable sex appeal. He reached into his pockets as solace for having survived an expected beating, where he fumbled about and came upon another piece of paper.

"What the hell? Where did this come from?" His fingers unfolded an unexpected note, like a character frozen amid some supernatural tale. "Maybe I do have Alfie's sex appeal, and this one of my secret admirer's love notes."

That turned out to be a fleeting fantasy, as the message read, "You don't belong here. Leave now." The words seemed to materialise from nowhere, only adding to his already unsettled psyche. He scanned the streets, searching for any sign of the messenger. The very air he breathed almost felt like it conspired against him. Was he being watched? Someone somewhere knew of his otherworldly origin and now urged him to return there. His imagination whirled like something from the depths of a Stephen King novel, as a chill of fear pulsed through his veins. The note became a harbinger of unseen terrors hiding in the shadows and had shaken his very essence to its core. The persistent stalker, whether a person or some more enigmatic entity, had pushed him over the edge. He could no longer linger in 2075. Equally unappealing, however, was the prospect of returning to 1975.

Steve decided in a fit of impulsive terror to return home in space, but not in time. The choice to visit 2023 was as random as tumbleweed in a deserted town; driven by the curious desire to glimpse Hometown within what he hoped would be his own lifetime.

With a clutch of newfound possessions, he retrieved the time machine and tinkered with the dials. One final, almost cavalier shake of the device, and Steve vanished into the unknown.

His disappearance did not go unnoticed, though, as a young, baffled child pulled on his father's arm. "Where did that man go?"

TEN

PREPARING FOR THE PAST

Steve had lived his whole life in one place and was well aware of Hometown's strengths and flaws. The opportunity now arose to benefit from foreknowledge and use devious street smarts to improve life once in the 20th century.

A plan formed to make the best use of his time in 2023. He'd noted several discussions about the Internet in 2075. It appeared to hold knowledge about everything. If it existed here, he would investigate historical sports results and reap the rewards back home. Of course, there would be more futuristic gadgets to collect as well.

The prospect of this second time travelling adventure overcame the fears he hoped to have left behind in the future.

The indelible desire to peer into his own future was forefront in his thoughts. What would become of the hopes and desires he now entertained?

Once more, he was starting from nothing in 2023, so it was time to make some money.

There had been easy pick-pocketing opportunities near the civic centre in the past. A few hours' work there would most likely create a similar result.

True to form, by 3pm there were eight wallets in his possession. It was like taking candy from a baby, but without the tantrums. With a soft touch and adept skill, no one ever suspected until he was long gone.

After distancing himself from the scene of the crime, he stopped to count his bounty. The total haul came to $25.30 in cash. He turned each wallet inside out and shook it. "How do people live around here? Perhaps they use some sort of device, like in 2075."

He had retrieved several plastic cards from the wallets, though. Some had the names of stores and others looked to be named after airlines. While others seemed to be visas with banks' names on them rather than countries. As in 2075, monetary matters confused Steve and he would have to learn by people watching.

After visiting a few shops, he thought he'd figured it out. With the ease at which plastic cards could buy stuff, and with over ten in his pocket, he gathered a mix of new and familiar items and sauntered over to the checkout to try out a card. In line, he saw the front-page story in a magazine with pictures of two guys that were arranging a fight. "I've met that guy. That's Elton, or Elen or something like that."

After nonchalantly swiping the card, he walked out of Publix. "This place is awesome!"

He decided 2023 was the time to be for a while and checked into a comfortable motel for the week, dropping everything in his room. The intention was to go back out, but travelling fifty-two years and several thousand miles had him exhausted. So, after watching Jerry Maguire, he soon fell into a fitful sleep.

With enthusiasm and vigour, Steve was up early the next morning, ready to shop for more futuristic fun to take home. Not being sure what was what and what did what, he entered an electronics store to look at the huge TVs and found some funky looking watches with apples, which went straight on his "To Buy" list.

A young assistant approached. "Heya! How can I help?"

"I'd like a watch with an apple."

"You mean an Apple Watch?" she asked.

"Do I? OK. As long as it tells the time." The beginnings of a frown formed on Steve's face.

"Anything else?"

"What do you mean, anything else? Your watches do tell the time, right?"

The conversation turned as the shop assistant opened Steve's mind to the multitude of uses watches could perform. His excitement level grew, his heart now racing, as the options became more and more outlandish.

"Yeah, OK. I'll have all those things."

"Cool. And you said you're an Apple man rather than an Android, right?" She saw by the look on his face that she'd lost him. "Well, if you want an Apple Watch, I'm guessing you already have an iPhone."

"What is all this about apples? What the hell are you talking about? I want my watch on my wrist, not stuffed in my mouth like a pig!" His embarrassment at looking like a total numbskull was obvious.

"No, an iPhone, and an Apple Watch. They talk to each other."

"Do they? What do they say?"

The junior assistant struggled to know how to continue. "Have you never heard of an iPhone before? Or Apple? How about Steve Jobs?"

"What jobs? Are you even speaking English?" Steve's voice cracked with frustration.

Confused, she called over a senior techy-type guy and handed over the difficult customer. He took Steve aside and spent the next half hour showing his own iPhone and Apple watch. Steve wanted all of it, despite not understanding terms like email, texting, Instagram and Google, but at the mention of The Internet, the sale was made.

With his iPhone and watch chosen, Steve trailed the guy to the checkout counter.

"That'll be $1,039.99 plus tax," the cashier announced, punching in the total on the EFTPOS.

Steve swiped one card and the EFTPOS machine displayed, "Please enter PIN."

With no clue what it was asking, he stood and waited.

The assistant, as pleasantly as possible, urged, "It needs your PIN number."

Steve feigned surprise. "Do I have to?"

"Er, yeah!" Sensing trouble, the young man scanned the store for a manager.

All Steve wanted now was a hasty exit. "I don't have it with me," he said. "I'll go grab it." Without a second thought, he bolted, his eyes fixed forward. However, his gaze soon locked onto a couple ahead who he'd seen purchase an iPhone and a watch. From a distance, he bided his time, knowing an opportunity would present itself.

Within a couple of minutes, they exited the mall, and Steve seized his chance. At a quickened pace, he caught them up, yanked the bag of goodies from their grasp, and darted down an alley. A wire fence loomed at the far end. Up and over it with ease, he vanished into the urban labyrinth beyond, leaving his victims distraught and unable to keep up.

Back at the motel, he sat on the bed and opened the boxes, excited to make use of all the features. He soon realised, though, that trying to figure out these two contraptions was impossible for him. Instead, he waited outside, looking for someone that appeared somewhat clever.

The only person around was a young pre-teen girl who seemed to have no inhibitions as she approached Steve. "I've never seen you before."

"No, you haven't. Well done." Steve wasn't sure why she started talking to him. But chatted with her while waiting for a genius to turn up that could help.

With her head buried in her phone, she inquired, "What you doing with that iPhone? Is that an Apple Watch? My dad has one of those."

"Where is your dad?" He hoped her dad might be nearby. "Would he know how to get these working?"

"How would I know? Haven't seen him since Christmas. I doubt he knows anything more than the basics about the iPhone 14 Pro or an Apple Watch Ultra." Words flowed from her mouth like some kind of child prodigy. She looked up. "But I do." And a smug grin lit up her face.

Steve offered her $5 to get them working and show him how they worked.

"You're kidding, right?" she said, her eyes once again fixed on her phone. "Fifty bucks and we can talk business."

"I don't have $50!" Her cocky attitude bringing a chuckle of disbelief to his voice.

"How much do you have?"

"Twenty bucks."

She looked up with a smirk. "Done. Hand it over."

Steve warmed to her unwavering confidence, handing over the cash.

Two hours later, he had an email address, had called KFC to order Wicked Wings and several photos and videos, including a panorama shot of the motel parking lot.

This Internet thing knew everything about everything and he learned how Google could find anything. Almost every place he visited asked for his email address, phone number, and home address. Steve's excitement soared as emails rolled in with offers of prizes and discounts and all you can eat buffets. So, the time had come to begin his "get rich soon" plan.

Back in 1975, the opportunities to make big money were few. The economy was in the doldrums after the recent oil crisis and only crime seemed to pay because no one else did.

By recording a variety of sports results from 1975, he figured there were huge rewards to be gained, especially from being so accurate. Sports betting was illegal back home, but he knew where to find underworld figures that would take his bets without question.

With everything penned in a little notebook, there was an overwhelming sense of anticipation. Excitement turned into a spur-of-the-moment decision, and within twenty minutes he was firing up the time machine. With the toys from his travels and the remaining Wicked Wings left behind, he returned to 1975.

ELEVEN

MESSING WITH THE MOB

Back home in time, but not in place, Steve scoured the bars of 26ᵗʰ Street, Chicago, hoping to find a bookie.

With cash from home and keen to use it, he struck up a conversation with a tall, tanned, snappy dresser and offered to buy him a drink. The guy's crooked nose was a distinctive contrast to the rest of his getup.

Steve decided he would palm himself off as some big shot from small town America. "I'd say you're a Chrysler kinda guy, for sure. You have the finesse and elegance."

This intrigued the stranger. "Yeah, I do have a soft spot for the plush seats in a spacious New Yorker. How'd you know that about me?"

"Could even be more of a Cordoba, with a personal and distinctive style." A cheeky grin crossed Steve's face. "And I bet you have a plush seat for the ladies too, right?"

Thirty minutes of sweet talking, along with several beers and a couple of single malts, and Steve was ready to take the dive. "Hey man, where can someone with cash to splash find a game?"

"What kinda game you looking for, friend?"

"I wanna lighten this load, burning a hole in my pocket by placing some bets. You know anyone interested?"

Over annunciating his words, the guy said, "Absolutely! Let's take a walk."

They soon hung a left and stopped in front of a solid metal door. Steve knew about petty crime but was about to immerse himself in organised crime. The stakes were much higher, and having come this far, he'd either end up a rich man or a dead one. Once inside the tobacco-hazy room, the immediate insecurity of being in over his head led to the decision to maintain a low profile. A cigarette made sure that wasn't to be the case.

He noticed a poster depicting the classic tortoise and hare race. It labelled the tortoise as 'Your odds of winning' and the hare as 'Your odds of explaining your losses to the wife.' The mix of smoke-filled lungs and stifling laughter brought on a coughing fit, which made him conspicuous, and now everyone was looking at him.

"Hamish!" Steve's newfound friend knew the owner. "My buddy here wants to test his luck. He's hunting for a Sportsbook."

A rotund, red-haired Irishman waddled over with a hearty demeanour. "Any pal of yours, Johnny, is a pal of mine," he said, placing his meaty hands on Steve's shoulders and peering into his eyes. "Let's get this game started, sonny boy!"

Steve tested the waters with a false bravado. "Can you handle this bet? I've got a hunch on the NASCAR Firecracker 400 — Richard Petty in first, Buddy Baker second, and Dave Marcis third. Here's my five."

Hamish raised an eyebrow but maintained his composure. "Well, ain't you the confident one?" he said with a chuckle. "Sure, we can take that action. No problem. I'll give you 50-1. Anything else I can assist ya' with?"

Steve continued his nonchalant act. "Anything else? Alright, how about we talk MLB? Put my winnings on the Nationals beating the Cardinals 5 to 1. And while you're at it, the Cubs taking down the Pirates 6 to 1."

Hamish's grin faded. "You're pushing your luck, buddy. But you got guts. Best I can offer is 20-1 if both come through. Take it or leave it."

Steve's mix of outward bravado and inward lack of confidence stopped him for a second, as though caught in headlights, but responded with, "I'll take it."

Hamish gave a wry smile. "Anything else, or would you like to guess my shoe size while we're at it?"

Steve, without thinking, shot back, "A lady's size six." Johnny spurt out a mouthful of beer, drenching Hamish's shoes.

Hamish's mood turned less than amicable. "You'd better be off. Come back after the fun and games end."

Steve was keen to be outside after struggling with the acrid smoke. He planned to place more bets somewhere else, hopefully without annoying the locals.

The 'L' train out to Elmwood Park provided a welcome change of pace. The area had a heavy Italian influence, and his flamboyant personality gelled with the local vibe. On this summery afternoon a warm breeze rustled the leaves overhead, carrying with it the faint notes of Italian ballads on an accordion. Men, young and old, couldn't resist the opportunity to flirt with beautiful ladies dressed in vibrant florals, pastel hues and light fabrics, many with sun hats and oversized sunglasses. This celebration of neighbourhood life stood amidst the backdrop of a sunlit suburban oasis.

It wasn't long, however, before Steve found the seedier side. He entered a smoky, dimly lit bar with checkered tablecloths and Sinatra playing in the background. Murmurings of a Sportsbook came from middle-aged Italian men engaged in animated conversations. He introduced himself as Benny from out east, before offering a round of drinks. Everyone was sceptical until he pulled a genie out of the bottle with an unbelievable story.

"It was early 1971," he began. "I was living in New York City and Ol' Blue Eyes was still the undisputed king of the music world in my book. Now, I wasn't much of a singer, but I was a huge fan, like everyone else. And as fate would have it, I found myself in a situation that I never imagined possible.

I was having a drink at one of those classic Manhattan bars. You know, the kind with cool lighting and the clinking of glasses in the background. The place had a timeless charm, kind of like Sinatra himself. Whilst sipping my bourbon, I noticed a commotion.

There he was, the Chairman of the Board in person, sitting a few stools away.

Of course, Sinatra loved a good drink. But on this night, he seemed to have overindulged a bit. He was slurring his words, stumbling around, and getting himself into a real mess. It was clear he needed some help.

I couldn't stand by and watch one of my idols embarrass himself like that. So, I mustered up the courage, walked over, and offered my assistance. I said, 'Mr. Sinatra, it's an honour to meet you. Is there anything I can do to help you get back to your hotel safely?'

He looked at me, those famous blue eyes blurrier than their usual piercing selves, and mumbled something about needing a cab. I waved one down, got him inside, and gave the driver clear instructions to take him to his hotel. I made sure he had everything he needed, and he left.

Now, I can't say for sure what would've happened if I hadn't stepped in that night, but I like to think I helped him avoid an embarrassing situation. And maybe, just maybe, I saved Sinatra's reputation that evening."

It must have been Steve's delivery, because they all appeared to buy the entire story, hook, line, and sinker. He became the life of the party and turned the conversation back to the Sportsbook he'd heard mentioned.

A reserved member of the group, with an air of sinister confidence enhanced by greying slicked back hair, touched his arm. "How much do you have in mind?"

"I can offer you fifty bucks on a trifecta of MLB games tomorrow. And if you like, I'll throw in the result of the Wimbledon tennis."

"Sure, young Benny from out east. Show me the money and tell me who will win."

The charismatic young man reached inside his pocket. "I'll tell you more than just the winner. I'll give you exact scores!" His head bobbed in the same arrogant comedic way Ali did when talking about George Foreman.

"Go ahead. I'm listening. In fact, write everything here."

Steve had it all memorised. Guardians 12 – 2 Red Sox; Yankees 2 – 5 Orioles; Phillies 10 – 7 Mets and Arthur Ashe was a talented African American that no one expected would beat the favoured Jimmy Connors. However, he wrote "Ashe wins 6-1, 6-1, 5-7, 6-4"

"That's some accumulator! And what odds are you expecting?"

Steve's eyes narrowed. "I'll take 200-1."

They discretely swapped $50 for a slip of paper and shook hands.

"If you win, of course, I expect you to buy us all another round of drinks."

"If I win, I'll buy the bar!" The entire group roared with laughter as a second round of drinks on Steve arrived.

After a few more tall stories and a fair amount more drinking, he left for the night. The trepidation of trying to collect the winnings from the mob without losing body parts tempered his relief at having placed the bets. A plan was forming, although he guessed chances were he wouldn't get away with it. But for Steve, life's fun derived from beating the odds.

Next day he was quick to rise, riding the 'L' train back to 26th Street amidst the bustling morning rush. From the moment he set foot on the train, he sowed the seeds of a rumour that spread like wildfire. As he neared the end of his journey, an electric anticipation filled the air, and he knew his scheme was taking root, at least for now.

A multitude of participants was essential to pull this off. With every caution thrown to the wind, he traversed the local market, cafes and businesses, even engaging in casual chats with newspaper vendors. Everywhere he went, the same rumour stoked flames of expectation that were about to become a full-on blaze.

He made his way to the unassuming metal door down the alley, the same one Johnny had led him to the day before.

Inside was as smoky and unwelcoming as before, and his gut screamed to leave, for several reasons. But he knew better than to show his hand and instead located Hamish across a sea of eager gamblers.

Their previous meeting had left Hamish seething, but now, his loathing for Steve reached boiling point. A master of the long game, Hamish understood the delicate balance he needed to maintain. Right there, he had to settle a debt, which meant handing over a cool $5,000.

Steve observed as the cashier counted out the money. Meanwhile, the heavies placed around the room eyed Steve like they were measuring him for a coffin. He had only been inside for fifteen minutes when he glanced at the wall clock; it read one minute to ten – his appointed time to bid farewell to his hosts.

The exit beckoned, and he made a beeline for it, trailed by four brawny goons, their intentions clear as day. As the metal door swung open, Steve stepped outside into a throng of hundreds, all clamouring, "It's 10am! Show me the money!"

He waded into the crowd and flung a handful of $5 bills into the air, right in the path of his hulking pursuers. The surge of human bodies swallowed the four would-be assailants, and pandemonium erupted. Bodies, limbs, and fists flew in all directions. A prosthetic leg even became wedged in the doorway of the gambling den, while stout middle-aged men and a few equally formidable women, armed with hefty handbags, emerged as the victors of the chaos.

Steve's audacious plan had worked like a charm. Amidst the utter bedlam, no one could make sense of anything, affording him a swift escape. He sprinted away as fast as his legs would carry him, not daring to look back until he had distanced himself by at least five blocks. After endless side streets and scaled walls, he knew it was time to return to Elmwood Park and collect even more dubiously earned gains.

The high-stakes game of deceit he was playing could well cost him his life, but for now, it had paid off handsomely, fuelling his confidence that he could pull it off again.

After such a crazy morning, he spent the rest of the day lying low. Preparations for what would eventuate the following day filled his thoughts, where he knew even greater winnings awaited.

When the next morning arrived, Steve walked the few hundred yards from his hotel to the bar. It was empty apart from a young man readying the place for punters.

"Where are the old guys?"Steve asked.

All he received was a blank stare and a shrug of the shoulders, which only brought frustration. So, he hung around in the hope that someone would turn up soon.

No one turned up at all; not for hours. Patience was not Steve's greatest virtue. In fact, it wasn't a virtue he possessed whatsoever.

About to walk away, he spotted a slight gentleman across the road beckoning him over. They walked a couple of blocks before entering a chic clothing shop. Through a curtain at the back, they transitioned into a labyrinth of corridors. The gentleman stopped at a door, knocked, and it opened.

In a smoke-filled room, Steve came face to face with the guy that had taken his bet.

Guiseppe was an old-style mobster, known for his sharp wit and shrewd judgment. Tension hung thick in the air as Steve took a gulp and figured out how he would leave with the full $10,000 in cash.

With a confidence that bordered on audacity, he leaned forward, his eyes locked onto those of the mobster, and acknowledged that reputation and honour were two of any man's greatest attributes. "Guiseppe, you possess these in droves," he said, trying to pull off his con by not only legitimising his predictions but also himself. "Listen," Steve started, his voice low and steady, "I've got something special, something inexplicable. It's a gift, you could say."

The mobster arched an eyebrow, his scepticism obvious. "A gift, huh? You better have something mighty convincing, kid."

Steve nodded; his expression unwavering. "I can predict the unpredictable. I've done it before. You've seen me do it once and I'll do it again."

The wily old mafia boss' curiosity got the better of him. "Alright, kid, I'll bite. Show me what you got."

Steve made a series of predictions for later that day: Orioles losing to the Yankees 6 to 1, The Indians nudging out the Red Sox 11 to 10 and Foolish Pleasure beating Ruffian in the head-to-head 11th race at Belmont.

Scepticism transformed into a mixture of awe and disbelief. "If you're right about Foolish Pleasure, you have a place here beside me. If that's true, it's worth more than money to me. I have been arguing all week with my daughter about that one."

Steve leaned in, his voice barely above a whisper. "I'm here to help you win big, my friend. With me on your side, you can clean up, with more cash than you ever thought possible."

Guiseppe leant backwards and opened a safe hidden beneath the floorboards, counted $10,000 in cash, and placed it on the table.

"Alright, kid," the mobster grumbled, "you've convinced me. Let's see if you're the real deal."

Steve scooped up the money, trying not to grin whilst exuding an air of victory. "You won't regret this. I'll meet you back here tomorrow, same time. Once you see that I'm 100% bang on correct, you're gonna want to do business." He stood to leave.

Giuseppe wasn't ready to let him go. "Sit!" Two hulking figures strong-armed him back into his seat. "No need for violence. Please sit. Please. I ask only one thing. Anyone that wins big with me, they arm wrestle my nephew, Tony. Loser buys the next round."

Steve took one look at the 6 foot 4 inch tall Italian Stallion. Tony looked impressive physically, but thinking he could beat him mentally, Steve said, "I'm game."

After five minutes of barely any movement, Tony was telling his life story to Steve, who, drenched in sweat, tried so hard not to lose. By this time, no one other than the two of them cared who would win.

Even Giuseppe lost the will to live. "OK, that'll do."

"No, Uncle Giuseppe! I have him right where I want him. I need one more minute."

Giuseppe slapped him around the ear. "Go turn on the TV."

The ninth race at Belmont flickered to life on the screen, and they all placed their bets. As luck would have it, Steve lost his wager, casting doubt on his abilities. However, when faith was wearing thin, a miraculous turn of events occurred in the tenth race. Steve's pick emerged victorious, reigniting their belief.

When Foolish Pleasure triumphed in the head-to-head, a satisfied Giuseppe nodded. "See you tomorrow, kid. See you tomorrow." A wave of the hand and Steve was off.

He couldn't shake the feeling that Giuseppe might decide to have him "taken care of" minutes after leaving with so much cold, hard cash. So, as soon as he was out of sight, he used his time machine to go back a couple of days and appeared in Hometown, where he made a discrete deposit of $14,525 into his bank account.

With that detour completed, he once again embarked on his journey, returning to 2023.

TWELVE

DESCENT INTO DESPAIR

Saturday 24th June 2023, 9pm, Hometown

One thing consumed Steve's thoughts after a few days away. How many emails did he have?

There were already thirty. Most were in the junk area. However, Steve considered them to be anything but junk. Many sought his attention with promises of wealth and Russian women seeking American companions for exciting exploits.

He relaxed on the bed, opened the minibar, and began responding to people worldwide, whilst finishing the Wicked Wings. With each drink and each reply, the world shrank, somehow. People seemed so friendly, which he attributed to the ease of communication. He was dying to hear from them all. But at that moment his inner voice, tanked up on liquor, sensed a late-night stroll calling his name and he ventured outside.

The following morning started with no great rush. His recollection of the night before was sketchy, but involved several new friends standing in a square, all of whom seemed stiff and motionless.

Electronic noises and pretty lights became annoying, so he threw stones at them until they stopped, after which he was so tired and dizzy, he returned to the motel.

With one hundred and fifty-seven emails waiting, too many before breakfast, he asked reception for food options. There was Starbucks, IHOP and Dunkin Donuts. All sounded like top of the range choices to him.

"Do people often bring food back from the store?"

"Yes, some. It's within easy walking distance. Why do you ask?" The receptionist gave him a strange look.

"You have a ramp for the trolleys."

"That's for wheelchairs."

"Ah, cool!" Steve's head wobbled as he steadied himself.

Starbucks took his fancy, and on reaching the front of the line, he placed his order. "A coffee and a bagel, please." The conversation that ensued took a while and confused the hell outta Steve, as he only knew about black and white coffee. So, after delaying what looked like half the town's population, he'd swiped yet another of the cards, and was outside sipping on an iced blonde caffe americano.

The chance to people-watch from his vantage point on a park bench, brought his attention to two young women sitting on a wall nearby. With a casual sip, out came a classic move. A nonchalant lean across the bench, followed by flashing an enigmatic grin that hinted at intrigue, faltered their conversation. They locked eyes with Steve, that smile inviting curiosity. Without saying a word, he gestured toward the space on the wall beside them. The women exchanged glances and, drawn in by his charisma, nodded in agreement. After introductions, he asked if the disco on Main Street was still open and whether they'd like to go for a boogie tonight.

"I've never seen a disco anywhere." The derision in their voices was obvious. "How long is it since you were last in town?"

"You wouldn't believe me if I told you. The place has changed a lot though since I was last here. There were never many Indians here before. Now the place is full of them."

"Indians? I don't see many Indians or Asians or many other foreign nationals, for that matter."

"No, Indians. Like on TV? You know, like The Lone Ranger's friend, Toto."

"That's not very PC! Don't you mean Native Americans?" one of them asked. "And his name was Tonto. Even I know that!" she quipped.

"I guess so. I've always called them Indians. Well, if there's no disco, what is there to do?"

"You could come with us to the culinary club. We are going there now."

He had no clue what a culinary club was. "Sure. I'd love to."

They arrived at a packed-out community hall, as the meeting was about to start. In search of seats, they passed the chatting throng of eager foodies, finding some in the front row. As soon as they sat down, the Japanese fish preparation demonstration began.

This wasn't Steve's kind of thing, but his motivation for coming was the girls. Sat beside one of them, he thought he'd test the waters and whispered something sweet into her ear. He got no reaction. So, in a faux display of shock, his hand ended up on her thigh and he turned and smiled.

"Have you never heard of #MeToo?" came the rebuke in an instant. With discretion and leaving no doubt in Steve's mind, she added. "Leave me alone! I will not tell you again! Next time you will feel pain."

Steve sat motionless. It was like he'd been slapped across the face with a fish. He squirmed in his chair as a warm flushed feeling turned him red. With nothing else to entertain him, he took an interest in the culinary demonstration, which now dealt with the fileting of meat. He found the ease with which the fancy-looking knife cut through flesh fascinating.

When the whole thing was over, he stood and, along with others, approached the table. With single-minded determination, he slipped the special knife up his sleeve and, having already decided the women were not his type, navigated his way through the crowd and left.

His mind focused on one thing: his phone. The idea of carrying the phone had not dawned on him, but as soon as he was back in his room, he picked up his new favourite toy and checked the messages. There were hundreds of emails, and with great delight, he clicked on everything and replied to almost every single one.

With the sense of belonging his newfound hobby brought, he was curious to find if anyone missed him when he disappeared in 1975. Google would have the answer.

There was next to nothing. He found a missing person report from July 1975, but other than that, he was a nobody. The missing person's report never led to a search, so he surmised no one had missed him. A heavy cloak of loneliness swept over him, as he wondered whether his temporal pursuits were his only genuine achievement in life.

In solace, nostalgia hit, as the memory of his brief visit to 1930 flashed through his mind. The gorgeous woman he'd met entered his thoughts, and he racked his brain to remember her name, but it wouldn't come to him until, with a face filled with soap suds in the shower, it hit him. "Joyce Tuttle!"

A site called ancestry.co.uk seemed to be the way to find out about her. He found a Joyce Tuttle from Liverpool and around the right age for the woman he'd met. Further down, he noticed something of particular interest. She had a son named Joseph, whose date of birth was Thursday 11th December 1930; nine months after their tryst at the dance.

Steve was gobsmacked!

Only one thought ran through his mind. He had to return to Liverpool and meet his son.

Google had been a mixed bag for Steve, and his emotions ran wild. He grabbed a few items, picked up his travel devices, and was gone.

Sunday 4th May 1941, 10.31am, Liverpool

Steve thought that travelling back almost a hundred years would have no effect on his emotions. Once he arrived, he was as determined to find his son as ever. After that, he'd figure out what to do next.

The search for Joseph would not be easy. Liverpool was a big city. His only choice was to walk and see who or what was around. Maybe he could meet people who knew someone that could lead him to Joyce. It was a long shot, but what else did he have?

He materialised beside the River Mersey, in an area he remembered well. After scraping together some clothing, he ventured beyond the dockside. The familiarity ended there.

That single visit, eleven years earlier, wasn't enough to navigate what now remained of the city. Bombs hadn't yet fallen from the sky. Within a few hundred metres, he began experiencing the utter devastation of building after building reduced to piles of rubble. Plenty of people were still out and about, living their lives as normally as possible. Steve walked, looking up and down each road and side street he came across, unsure of where to go or what to do.

It hadn't been thirty minutes before, against all odds, his greatest wish came true. On the opposite side of the road, a woman with long red hair walked towards him. Was it her? He froze in disbelief. It was indeed. Not knowing what to say or do, he used the iPhone to snap a photo to at least have something to remember her by. With head bowed, he passed by, as she walked arm in arm with an older man. He wasn't yet ready to meet her face to face.

Twenty paces past, he turned to look. Beside her was a boy who he estimated to be ten or eleven years old. Emotions he'd never known surfaced. Was it pride or love or something else? He didn't know.

There was no chance they were leaving his sight. And when the time was right, he would talk with Joyce and hopefully meet his son.

Steve was no P.I. and had no experience of following undetected. He kept what he thought to be a safe distance, but when they jumped on a tram at James Street, he was in danger of losing them. All he could do was to run. The cause looked to be lost until a taxi appeared, which he hollered, before slumping into the backseat, and the chase continued. "Follow that tram!"

"Are you visiting? You sound American." The driver was keen to chat.

"You're right on both counts. I'm here with a secret weapon to help you Brits win the war." Steve decided to have some fun. "You see this?" He took out the iPhone. "This will take photos, play music, send and receive messages and it'll make phone calls."

"Careless talk costs lives! You sure you're meant to be telling me all that?"

"Yeah, man. Don't worry. Be happy." Steve knew those words from somewhere, but couldn't pinpoint their source.

The taxi was a godsend as Joyce remained on the tram for twenty minutes. Even Steve's long legs could not have kept up.

"OK, they're off. Thanks. Stop here."

"That'll be three bob, please."

"Er…I don't have…You know what? Take this."

Steve exited the backseat and moved in beside the driver, handing him the iPhone. The driver was unsure, but accepted it and deposited the phone in his jacket pocket. He went to shake Steve's hand to wish him well, but Steve leaned over and gave him a big hug. As fast as he'd sat down, though, he was up and off and after Joyce on foot.

Her group walked for several minutes before entering a family home. Steve needed to remain in touch without drawing suspicion. Seated at a park bench over the road from where the house was visible, he reached into his jacket pocket to check for his iPhone. The driver's wallet was also in there, as it popped out at the same time he was retrieving the phone.

Then it rained. He'd done his best to find appropriate clothes, but rain hadn't been in his plans. As water leaked through the top of the coat and down his back, now cold and a touch lonely, Steve's mood turned. "What am I doing in World War Two England, drenched and freezing?"

There were no cafes, but there was a pub nearby. So, he sauntered over to drown his sorrows in a few pints of English beer.

The longer he sat there drinking beer after beer by himself, the fouler his mood became. And after the barmaid slapped him for misuse of his hands, he was told to leave.

Steve stumbled out into the cold, wet early evening just in time to see that Joyce had walked past a few seconds earlier. He almost approached them on the spot, but in his haste, tripped and fell.

Back on his feet, he remained at a distance until the older guy entered one house and Joyce and the boy went next door.

This was the opportunity Steve had come all this way for. He gave it five minutes before staggering forward and knocking on the door.

A friendly young boy opened the door. "Mum, there's a man at the door."

Steve stood shivering, with his arm perched against the doorframe for support. "Are you Joseph?" he said, with eyes transfixed on the youth before him.

"Joe. Who are you?"

Before Steve could answer, Joyce saw him and stumbled.

Joe turned and rushed to his mother's aid. "Mum! You OK?"

Joyce regained her composure and approached the doorway, trying not to show weakness. "I saw you on The Strand earlier. How is it possible that you haven't aged a day in eleven years? Where have you been all this time?" Her eyes darted around, looking at Steve, the ground and across at Joe. "No, I don't want to know."

"Can I come in?" Steve asked in a slurred voice. "Even if for only a few minutes."

"Who's he, Mum?" Joe looked first at his mother before turning to look up at Steve, the cogs of realisation turning inside his brain.

"OK, you can come in," Joyce said, ushering him into the lounge. "Joe, get a towel, please."

When Joe returned, Joyce sent him to play in his room. A little upset at not having his question answered, he obeyed.

Steve didn't beat around the bush. "Is he my son?"

"Yes. Joe is your son, biologically. But you're certainly not his father." Steve sensed years of hurt surfacing for Joyce.

"What does he know about me?"

"What's it to you?" Her firm but hushed voice remained out of Joe's earshot. "What difference does it make after so long?"

"It makes a difference to me."

"I don't give a damn what matters to you! He's my son and I will decide what matters!"

Those words burned deep into Steve's psyche. The simmering tension now boiled up as his fist lashed out, knocking her to the floor.

"Don't tell me that I don't matter! Do you hear me?"

Joyce looked shocked at the sudden violence, but not one to cower in the face of aggression, she snapped back, "You don't matter. You never did. You were a five-minute fling ten years ago and nothing more than a lousy lay!"

If the punch was the entrée, the beating he was now prepared to unleash would be the main course. His right leg came at her with a vicious ferocity that would have incapacitated her, except Joyce used a nearby chair as a shield, and he kicked that instead. Steve lost his balance and grabbed at a lamp for support, but pulled it down upon himself as he collapsed in a heap.

Joyce took the opportunity to clamber to her feet, searching for a weapon to defend herself. Nothing in the lounge seemed adequate, so she ran into the kitchen.

"Where's the cleaver? I need the damn cleaver!" Pots and pans flew as a frantic search ensued. She fumbled around in a drawer. "Ah! Found it!"

Her head turned to check on Steve, only to find his face, full of fury, filled her vision. With a shrill scream, she hurriedly turned back to grab the cleaver, as Steve pressed his body against hers.

Joyce began to swing her weapon, but a sudden sharp, deeply penetrating pain in her abdomen, consumed every part of her being. A yell of desperation wiped the grimace from Steve' face, as he stepped back and withdrew the Japanese fileting knife from her belly.

"I want to look, but I'm afraid." Joyce's hushed voice was now the solitary sound as she turned her head downwards. With pain etched across her face, she watched a dark spot on her torn clothing become a rapidly growing crimson stain. Her trembling hands covered the injury. However, within seconds, she collapsed to the floor and her breathing became laboured.

In the moment, Steve's mind and body shook, unsure whether he had intended to create the gruesome result before him.

The sound of Joe running down the stairs snapped him out of a trance. He threw the knife on the floor and ran to intercept him before he reached the room. With his unbloodied arm, he took Joe by the wrist to pull him away from the gruesome scene.

"Get off me!" Joe wriggled and writhed.

Steve's grip tightened. "Your mum needs some time alone. Come on, let's take a walk." He manhandled Joe away from the kitchen and out the back door, which slammed behind them. He tried hard to wipe the blood off his hand before asking Joe if he could show him the neighbourhood so his mother could rest.

Hesitant but compliant, Joe agreed, and they walked out the back gate.

Steve was ready with the next stage of his off-the-cuff decision-making.

While in the pub, he'd set the coordinates for 1986. It hadn't been his intention to return with his son, but not everything in life goes as planned.

A minute after shutting the gate, they vanished…together.

THIRTEEN

GREED IS GOOD

Joe's life had been a struggle thus far, including two years of war, but adversity had built resilience. If he'd had stayed in 1941, they would have evacuated him from Liverpool, which would have meant separation from his mother for a reason. Instead, Steve's arrival led to isolation from her, with no knowledge or understanding of why.

Joe's transportation to a foreign land at a foreign time was, therefore, a tremendous shock to one so young.

Steve turned towards Joe. "Wasn't that fun?"

The expressionless void on Joe's face told Steve nothing.

"Joe!" Shaking the boy's shoulders brought no response. "Snap out of it, son!" There was little for Steve to do other than check into a motel and care for him, hoping his demeanour would change.

Steve decided not to risk walking about town too much, having lived there all his life. So, at the first opportunity, he withdrew some of the Chicago funds, bought a rickety old pickup and drove out of town for seclusion. Way out in the woods and hills, the earthy aroma of damp soil combined with the sweet perfume of wildflowers, and the faint, invigorating tang of pine.

Joe grew up in dense housing surrounded by more dense housing. This was an adventurous new experience that drew him out of his shell a bit at a time. He still did not know who Steve was, but without other options, followed his lead. The ability to adapt was a great strength as his confidence increased daily. Within a week he seemed a different person, from outward appearances, and spoke for the first time.

"Where's my mum?" Joe asked, his eyes and his voice sunken in sadness.

"Has your mum ever talked about your dad?"

"Not at all. She said we were good, just the two of us." Joe bowed his head. "So, I never asked."

"How interested are you in finding out about him?"

"It would have been nice to at least know something about him. Right now, though, I want my mum."

Steve knelt down before him. "Joe, this is going to sound strange, but I am your dad."

Joe's eyes widened, his young mind clearly struggling to process the news. After blinking a few times, took a step back and studied this apparition. "You're my dad?" His voice wavered with a mix of surprise and confusion.

Steve nodded, his expression filled with hope and apprehension, before extending a hand. However, he stopped short, unsure how the young boy would react. "This is a lot to take in. I didn't know about you until recently. Your mum and I... well, there's lots to explain."

As both peered into the other's eyes, Steve assumed Joe searched for signs of deception. "Why'd you leave us?" Joe's curiosity outweighed the uncertain tone of his voice.

Steve sighed, realising the weight of the situation. "It's not that simple, Joe. There were circumstances I couldn't control. But I regret not being around all these years."

Tears welled up in Joe's eyes. "I never even thought about you before now."

Steve placed a hand on Joe's shoulder. "I want the chance to get to know you and be part of your life."

Joe nodded, still processing everything. "I guess we could give it a go. But I need to talk to Mum."

Steve had grappled all week with deep regret and the enormity of his actions, but also contemplated how he would tackle Joe's questions. Anxiety and fear that Joe would somehow learn about Joyce's demise and reject him burnt a knot in his stomach. "Why don't we focus on getting used to this new place? I'll show you around, and we can talk more about everything else later."

With that, they packed up and left the dingy motel to upgrade to a log cabin.

Joe struggled to reconcile the stranger before him with the father he'd imagined over the years. Doubts and questions gnawed at his mind, leaving him with a sense of unease.

In the following weeks, they hiked through hills, discovered hidden waterfalls and caves, and swam in pristine lakes, which caused everything on their bodies to shrivel. One evening, the tall grass in the meadows was ideal for lying back in, and for the father to identify constellations for his son. Like explorers of the wild and stewards of their natural sanctuary, their appreciation of the outdoors helped forge a bond; a testament to the healing power of nature.

One gorgeous Wednesday morning, before the sun was up, Steve and Joe, armed with rods, a wicker basket, and Joe's desire to smoke fish, followed a worn trail through the woods down to a secluded lake.

At the water's edge, they practised casting, each watching their bobbers with anticipation. The minutes passed with only the gentle lapping of the water and the symphony of birds for company. With the chance to talk in such peaceful surroundings, Joe expressed his feelings. Out came all his emotional turmoil, being overwhelmed and confused by his sudden life shift; the sense of loss and abandonment caused by being taken from his mother. He longed to see her, to hear her voice, and to be held close. The separation was a painful wound that seemed impossible to heal.

Yet, amidst the chaos of his emotions, Joe was also curious. He couldn't deny a flicker of intrigue about this new world. The log cabin, the lakes, the hills, and the meadows held a particular fascination. But most of all, the opportunity to live in the future created a desire to learn.

Joe's bobber dipped beneath the surface, and his eyes widened with excitement. Together, they reeled in their first catch—a gleaming trout. The joy on Joe's face was palpable. However, Steve hadn't expected to catch anything, and hoped they wouldn't, as he feared slimy living creatures touching him.

"Get it away from me!" Steve screamed.

"Your voice turns girlie when you're scared." Joe paused and allowed the fish to flop around a bit more on Steve's lap, but once he could no longer hold in his laughter, the hilarity burst out and he grabbed the fish.

For Steve, the outdoors life was about being one with the earth, but animals were a different kettle of fish, so to speak. Joe ensured Steve got the full experience, though, as he mishandled the fish, which flopped up onto Steve's lap once again. Steve ran a mile while Joe almost wet himself, laughing.

Joe continued to fish, catching one more trout before walking to where Steve was hiding and back to the truck. They drove home on the old dusty road, arriving in good time to cook the fish for breakfast, the shared adventure and Steve's vulnerability helping build a sense of camaraderie.

Throughout their few months in 1986, Steve had sought to make a fortune from his 2023 learnings. The 1980s seemed to be full of get rich quick schemes while stock market prices shot up. Millionaires emerged from a budding tech industry like cockroaches from a dark pipe. He'd believed that if you knew where to look, you'd make big money. Except, despite having foreknowledge, Steve struggled to grow his winnings.

That changed once he found his Apple Watch. It no longer worked, but triggered an idea. Out of curiosity, he made an enquiry as to Apple's share price.

"Twelve cents!" Steve's mind whirled with the possibilities. He had seen how popular Apple products were in 2023. "Surely," he thought, "they must be worth a fortune in 2023."

He made enquiries and bought $10,000 of twelve cents shares.

Once the share certificates arrived, Steve was ready to leave. "Joe, I want us to live in 1975 where I am from. But for right now, how about we travel further into the future?"

Joe looked up and pointed at a movie billboard. "How about we go Back To The Future?"

"That looks kinda cool. Yeah, let's see that first."

"Is that in colour, like those TVs we've seen?" They didn't have a TV in their cabin, but Joe loved watching them in shop windows.

"Yep, in colour."

Joe had never visited a cinema before, so the movie posters and smell of popcorn enthralled him. The size of the screen, though, grew his eyes to be as big as baseballs. With a bucket of popcorn, he sat in silence, glued to every second of the movie. As the credits rolled, Joe thanked Steve with a broad smile and a big hug.

"We should go outside so we can continue our own adventures through time." Steve led the way, searching for a secluded spot for their temporal shift.

"Joe," a voice called from behind them.

Joe turned, his face looking like he'd seen a ghost. But before he could speak, Steve had taken a swipe at the man, which landed full on the chin. A younger guy came at Steve with a couple of fearsome blows, making Joe recoil in fear. However, Steve barely seemed to notice them, hitting back so that both assailants were now on the ground. One of the men's wallets fell out of his back pocket and Steve swooped to gather it up, before grabbing Joe's arm and shouting, "Come on, run!" as they tried to avoid a second onslaught.

"I can't run any faster." Joe's bowed legs slowed him down. "They're coming!"

"OK, everything's set." Steve pulled Joe down a dark alley and, with a shake of the gadget, they were gone.

Monday 26th June 2023, 7.30am, Hometown

Steve thought they would appear in his motel room, but the reality was quite different. They materialised in the middle of a bustling road, nose-to-nose with a bewildered policeman who was struggling to direct traffic. The intersection's traffic lights got smashed two nights earlier, and the lazy Sunday that followed meant that no one repaired them.

In an instant, both men jumped backwards, narrowly avoiding a lip-smacking collision. "Where the Hell did you come from?" the policeman screamed, his flailing arms misdirecting traffic, causing a Chevy truck and a Ford Ranger to collide. The officer pointed at Steve. "You stay right there! Don't move!" He radioed for help and rushed to help the accident victims.

Steve wanted to help too…himself. He tugged on Joe, who was still out of breath. "Let's get outta here," he said, pulling Joe away from the chaos.

They retired to the motel to recover from all the exercise. "This damn contraption broke! I'm sure I had the settings right."

Once refreshed, Steve asked at reception for the Yellow Pages, but having not seen one for many years, the man behind the desk struggled to find one. Minutes later, a tattered Yellow Pages from 2016 arrived. Puzzled by the delay, Steve asked, "Are there any stockbrokers in there?" They found one and set off to find him.

Steve and Joe, dressed more for an 80s-themed shindig than a business meeting, walked into the office with an air of anticipation. "Can we see a stockbroker, please?"

The well-dressed receptionist asked, "Do you have an appointment?" Steve realised they may have wasted their time, but tried flirting as his eyes met hers and his voice softened. "No. I'm so sorry, we don't. Do we need one? May I say, you have such a beautiful and welcoming smile?"

"Mr. Fisher is a busy man," she said, rolling her eyes. "May I ask what this is concerning?"

Despite Steve's rejection, Joe interjected. "You may. We want to sell you some apples."

"We don't need any," her curt reply bringing a grimace to Joe's face.

At that moment, an older man, well passed retirement age, with a receding hairline, strolled in from an early lunch. "Any messages, Doreen?"

"No. None at all, Mr Fisher."

Fisher entered his office and closed the door.

"What are we, Doreen?" Steve leant over her desk and scowled, his eyes locked on hers, as if to change her mind using ESP.

"I think you should leave. I don't want to have to call security."

"You won't have to. We'll take our Apple certificates somewhere else." Steve's agitation was obvious as his voice grew louder.

In an abrupt twist, Mr Fisher's office door flew open. "Apple certificates? Physical share certificates on paper, you mean?"

"I do." Steve took the folded certificate out of his pocket.

"May I see them, please?" Fisher's whole body shook, causing Doreen's face to become flushed, having seen his nervous excitement.

"Holy Crap! How long have you had these? They look almost new. Come into my office. Doreen, hold my calls!"

Once all three cramped themselves into the office, Mr Fisher checked the Apple share price. He looked up for a moment and laughed. "You see that? Even with a finger missing, I type as fast as my secretary. Lost it trying to catch a Chilli Mango Jellybean that tried to escape out the car window."

"Did a passing car rip it off?" Steve asked, as Joe tripped over a chair, gripped in anticipation, awaiting the answer.

"Nothing that simple." Fisher scratched the back of his head. "I caught it at the very moment an eagle flew by and thought it was a snack worth fighting for. He got the Jellybean and my sticky finger." After a brief pause, he continued, "Moving on, I have good news and I have bad news."

"OK, give us the good news first." Steve stood to pace the room. "I'll ignore the bad news. Your lips will move, but in my head, I'll be singing 'Let's Get It On' or 'Sexual Healing' or something. I hate bad news. Marvin is my go-to for handling bad news. Yeah, I'll stop babbling now."

"I'll start with the bad news. You won't be able to sell these today."

Steve stopped pacing. "How bad is that? Is it like one day bad or one year bad? When can I sell the shares?"

"The certificate needs to be authenticated, as does your identity. Should take a couple of days."

Joe's pre-pubescent scouse voice blurted out, "Oh yeah? And what's the good news then, mister?"

Fisher stood, walked round the table and with a firm grip took hold of Steve's arms. "These are worth nearly $15,000,000."

Steve's legs buckled. "Do you mean I am going to be rich?"

"I would say so, yes. With my financial adviser hat on, to help with getting these authenticated and such, my fee would be just 1%. You'll still make $14.5million. Does that sound fair?"

"Yeah man! Sounds cool to me."

"Call me George."

Joe tugged on Steve's arm. "I need to talk to you."

"Do you need to pee?" Steve looked over at Fisher. "Is there a restroom?" He was keen for Joe to leave the room for a few minutes while the adults talked business.

But Joe was persistent and tugged on his arm again. "No, we need to talk outside. I'll tell you why out there." Joe's face mirrored the determination in his voice.

Steve relented, and they exited into the hallway for a private chat.

"That money's no good to us in 2023. We need it in 1975. Can you spend 2023 money in 1975?"

Steve's face went pale. "Hadn't thought about that. We need a way to get this money back to 1975."

"That's why you need me. I have. We need gold. Change this money into gold and we can take that back with us."

Steve's face lit up once more. "You're not just a pretty face, are you?"

"I'm not pretty! Don't call me pretty!"

Back with George, Steve asked, "Do you know how we can get some gold? As in several million dollars of the stuff."

"Gold should be one aspect of your overall portfolio, but not the whole thing. You want to diversify."

"No, gold will be fine. What do you think, little guy?"

"I think I'm relieved you didn't say I'm pretty again. And yeah, give us gold."

Joe's cheekiness amused George. "I can arrange for bullion to be purchased and stored in a secure vault for you."

"Let's do it, George. Can you make the arrangements?" Steve and Joe made it clear they were ready to leave.

George worked with a local bank, keeping the certificate safe in a deposit box until the shares sold and the cash converted into gold.

In the meantime, Steve had a few days to play with and a stolen wallet with which to enjoy them. There was a bunch of cash, but there were also a few plastic cards like he'd stolen during his last visit to 2023.

Steve took Joe out for Papa John's that first night. On finishing a Philly Cheesesteak pizza, he wanted pizza every night. As soon as he walked outside, though, he changed his mind.

"I want to go there tomorrow instead." Joe pointed at the picture of a bird on the restaurant across the street. "I love owls."

Steve agreed. They shook on it and returned to their hotel for the night.

They walked up to the entrance for lunch the next day, and Joe held the door open for Steve to enter. Steve walked in and thought he'd hit heaven. His mouth dropped, his eyes opened wide, and he took a step back to take in the entire room.

Joe pulled on his arm. "Why are you staring at all the waitresses?"

In an uncharacteristic decision, Steve grabbed Joe, turned him round and pushed him back out the door. "I'll come back by myself rather than have my style cramped by a kid."

"I won't cramp your style. Maybe you'll cramp my style if we go to Hooters together."

Steve had his mind set that flirting and kids don't mix, so searched for somewhere else to eat. "That's where we should go."

Joe struggled to resist Steve's incessant pushing, but looked in the direction Steve's finger indicated. "Perfect! It's got my name on it."

Seated at a booth inside Joe's Crab Shack, Steve's mindset soon changed as he noticed a tall staff member with long, blond hair walking away from him. "Hey gorgeous, I want the best there is for me and my son, Joe. What can you serve up?"

They turned and approached the table. "Hey guys. What's up? I'm Kenny. I'll be your server." Steve looked down, avoiding eye contact. "You want Feast of the Beast, man! There's crab cakes, blackened tilapia and shrimp. You get like, Joe's Classic Sampler and…"

"I want all that!" Joe's eyes were the size of saucers. "I've never heard of it, but if it looks like what he's eating," he pointed at the table beside them, "I'll give it a try."

"It comes with shark attack dessert, too."

Joe's lower jaw dropped. "What's a shark?"

"Yeah, right!" Kenny laughed and left to place the order.

The next hour involved Steve and Joe devouring every morsel placed before them. The mess on Joe's face and his ability to fit so much into his small body astounded Kenny. "Dude, where are you packing that away? Way to go, Joe!" He raised his hand in Joe's direction. "Don't leave me hangin'!"

Joe's expression transformed into a blank stare, before his infectious smile returned. "The crab and shrimp pasta was delicious.

Especially with tons of the red tabco sauce. I want to eat here all the time. I love this place."

Steve grabbed the bill. "Sure. We can talk about that later. Also, it's Tabasco, not tabco. And with the half bottle you just swallowed, there's a life lesson coming your way real soon." Steve wiped his mouth as he stood from the table. "Let's pay and get outta here."

At the cashier, he whipped out the card he'd used the day before and gave it a swipe.

"It says denied, sir." The young lady beckoned the manager over.

Steve heard her whisper, "It says failure code 43." The manager whispered something back to her, which Steve missed. She walked towards the back of the restaurant, out of their line of sight.

"May I help you with your credit card, sir? The manager reached out to grasp the card, but Steve withdrew.

"I'll pay by cash." The wallet came out. Steve threw money on the desk, grabbed Joe, and left. "Keep moving. Don't look back."

As fast as possible, they returned to their motel, only to notice from across the street two police officers at reception.

"That's them." The manager pointed in their direction.

"Taxi!" Steve shouted. Within ten seconds, away they went in a cab that soon had them lost in a labyrinth of side streets.

"These cards must be no good." He flung the cards out the window and lay back to relax. "Let's ditch them and use cash from now on."

They searched for new accommodation and it took a few attempts, but just as Joe's bowels kicked into overdrive, they found a place to stay that didn't insist on a credit card.

After several more days, the wallet was empty and everything was in place. George got paid and Steve and Joe were on their way to see their gold.

They were escorted to a secure room outside the vault. "How much gold would you like us to bring out for you today?"

"All of it." Steve wanted to get the gold and return with it to 1975.

"That will take a long time." Their escort's face remained unreadable. "That's a lot of gold. Are you sure you want to walk out of here with it all?"

Steve asked, "What does 1kg feel like?"

The bank man brought a 1kg bar and Joe felt its weight. "That's heavy! How are we going to carry over two hundred of these?"

Through trial and error, they decided 70kg was all they could carry. The happy, relaxed expressions they'd expected to don whilst leaving, were instead faces full of sweat and irritation, as they dragged two large suitcases into a taxi, which got off to a slow start, before taking them to a new plush hotel suite. Once inside, Steve knew he had to shake the time machine one last time. He'd achieved more than his craziest dreams ever imagined, and would always keep the devices. But, as he told Joe, "I may never use these again."

It was time to return home.

FOURTEEN

CHANGING LIVES

Conscience is a multi-layered element of any person's psychology. For the past few months, since killing Joyce in an act of uncontrolled rage, Steve had ignored every inkling of its existence. A darkness had grown within for which he was unprepared. Time travel had been the lucky break in life that he now intended to take full advantage of, but the familiarity of home was about to free the beast from its lair.

The mess of stolen items he'd left behind was still on his bedroom floor. He discarded them all. In fact, he discarded the entire apartment.

"Ignore the mess. We won't be here long. Hold this a second." Steve handed Joe a small velvet bag while he attempted to hide the gold under the bed. In his haste, some bars got stuck, which only frustrated him. With everything safely tucked away, they ventured out for breakfast.

Steve dived into his eggs and hash browns. "People know me around here and I don't have a son. We need a story for who you are."

"I could be your nephew." The absurdity of his idea hit home when he added, "From Liverpool."

Steve laughed. "We can make it work. It'll work to our advantage that you're from overseas. We should change your name, though. What's your middle name?"

"Brian," Joe said in a hushed voice, looking down at his feet.

Steve decided that was Joe's name now and moved on to discussing money matters. "I want three things: a Mustang; a big house, and I wanna fix and sell cars. We're gonna need financial advice about the gold and setting up a new business. Yellow Pages will help."

Joe, now Brian, wanted to know where he fit in. "You'll have to go to school," Steve said.

"Thought so." Brian finished his fifth piece of bacon, and they ambled back to the apartment.

First thing they did was to look under the bed. "We can't do anything about the gold until Monday, but it must not leave our sight in the meantime."

The rest of Saturday was torturous. So much wealth in their possession, yet patience was their only option.

Sunday arrived, and they were happy to wait it out. But then the doorbell rang.

"Stay quiet and ignore it." Steve put his finger to his lips.

"Steve! Come on! I know you're in there." Phil wanted to divvy up the loot from their burglary.

"I'm not here. I'm sleeping. Come back tomorrow." Steve gritted his teeth and waited to hear Phil's reaction.

"You have my bag. I need it."

"I'll bring it over tomorrow."

"Do you have a woman in there?" Phil's jealousy of Steve's success with women had often been a source of discord.

"Yeah. Now go away."

"That's never stopped you from letting me in before!"

"Oh, shut up!" Steve relented and allowed Phil inside. "This is my nephew Brian from England."

Phil nodded in acknowledgement. "And where's your lady friend?" His eyes scouring the place. "Is she hiding under the bed?"

Both Brian and Steve jumped in front of Phil before he could take a step in that direction.

"What's that about?" Phil stepped forward to search under the bed.

Steve pushed him backwards. "Don't!"

"Don't? I'm trying to look under the bed."

"Don't!" Steve pushed him harder.

A battle of wills soon turned aggressive. Neither would back down, and Steve's rage built until he smacked Phil with a right hook. The surprise, more than the punch, knocked Phil to the ground. He scrambled to his feet. Steve hit him again. "Stay down or go home."

"I'll go home. And you can consider our partnership, no, our friendship, over." Phil pulled himself up off the floor. "What is wrong with you?" He left Steve's house, promising to never return.

Brian huddled in the corner of the room, afraid to say or do anything, as Steve stood at the window, shaking and watching as Phil walked out of his life, forever.

Monday morning arrived as a relief for Brian, who was ready to deal with the gold. For Steve, however, he experienced the initial symptoms of grief, having lost Phil. He left Brian in charge of the gold and gave him the phone number of the financial adviser he'd chosen in town. "If anything happens, call that number and ask for me."

The air was brisk, as was Steve's pace, arriving right at 9am. He introduced himself to the young man at the front desk, and asked to see a financial advisor.

"I can see if Mr Johnson is free this morning. What is your name?"

"Steve Harding." Steve shook hands with the young man. "Oh look, you have all your fingers."

With a confused frown on his face, the young man replied, "Sorry, have we met before?"

"I'm not great with faces, but I never forget a voice. Good to see you again, George. Thanks for everything, and don't hold too tightly to those Jellybeans."

The innocent youth looked up at Steve, his head tilted and eyes squinting. "You're welcome, I think."

Steve raised both eyebrows. "You will be."

With meticulous arrangements in place to secure the gold's safe deposit, most of it was converted into a substantial $350,000 cash sum. The next day, Steve found himself behind the wheel of a 1975 Mustang II Mach 1, a sleek 2-Door Fastback that set him back $4,000 in cold, hard cash.

By week's end, three realtors were vying for his business, and a week later, one emerged victorious. Steve and Brian soon settled into a splendid three-bedroom, two-bathroom home; a haven complete with pool and charming little garden costing $67,500.

* * *

Brian began school, where he adapted to new surroundings, forged friendships, and even picked up an Irish American twang. Yet, in the solitude of his thoughts, his mind invariably wandered back to his mother, and the unwavering determination to uncover the truth.

His life experience was far broader than his peers. However, it gave him few advantages until the day he first met Tank, the eleven-year-old boy no one crossed, not even the teachers. This was Tank's first day at his third school this year. He saw Brian. He saw his shoes, and he decided they were now his shoes.

To go with his bowed legs, Brian had huge feet for his age, and he'd taken, without asking, Steve's Air Asics from 2075. They looked like any other shoe, which is how Steve wanted it to stay in public. Once they were armed, though, they lifted off the ground.

The last bell of the school day rang, and Brian hurried out of the gate, eager to get home early. But as loud footsteps closed in on him from behind, panic surged through his being. Tank approached, a wicked grin beaming across his face.

"Give me your shoes." His matter-of-fact manner was his most endearing quality.

Without waiting for a response, Tank lunged forward, reaching for Brian. With a swift leap, Brian activated the shoes, and, like magic, he was airborne, hovering just above Tank's grasping hands. Within seconds, a crowd gathered, watching in awe.

With Marty McFly as inspiration, he made his getaway, expecting to do it in style. Confident he could glide over a nearby pond, like Marty on his hoverboard, he sped towards the water. The shoes created a cushion of air that allowed him to bounce off the ground. Arrival at the pond was another story, though. He miscalculated how different it would be to bounce of water, slipped and face-planted, creating an enormous splash. Students burst into laughter, before an eerie silence fell upon the scene, as Tank came walking towards Brian. As wimpy as a willow, drenched and wearing bits of pond weed, Brian was in no state to argue with or defend himself. A bit of wee leaked out as he waited for the inevitable.

Tank walked out into the pond fully clothed, grabbed Brian by the collar, and pulled him up out of the water. "You're funny. I like you," he said in his endearing matter-of-fact way.

They extricated themselves onto dry land, side by side, as everyone watched in awe, from a distance.

Brian never had an issue with Tank again, who found he'd gained the respect of many of his peers for his actions that day. In fact, Brian and Tank hung out together until Tank was once more moved to another school for flattening a teacher.

After thanking Tank for pulling him from the pondweed, Brian bounded home, arriving early enough to fulfil a mission he'd set himself. Where were the elusive devices that were key to his return to 1941? A meticulous scouring of every nook and cranny came up empty. He could only surmise that Steve either kept them close at hand or secured them away from the only person aware of their existence.

* * *

Life was a whirlwind for Steve. A business partner had entered the picture, and together they ventured into the world of second-hand car sales, christening it Harding & Andersen Autos. Twin Motors or Doppelgänger Vehicles would have been quirkier yet appropriate, as many people had difficulty telling them apart. The likeness was how they met in the first place, coming second last and third last in an Elvis impersonation contest. The guy in last place was a better look-a-like, but his wig got knocked off whilst doing a windmill, halfway through Blue Suede Shoes.

Their enterprise took flight, and in six months, they had doubled the number of lots under their banner.

For Steve, life had never been more promising, and the benefits of wealth provided a lifestyle and possessions he'd only dreamt of whilst a thief. There were the watches and cars, plus a prized Glock pistol he'd read about years earlier, and now owned. Not only did he own it, but he also showed it off and left it lying around at home. When not in use, the barrel was always empty, despite its owner often being loaded.

Beneath the surface, however, lurked an insidious self-doubt, gnawing away at his confidence. For the first time in his life, Steve was without a stalwart supporter that he looked to when unsure or depressed. To steady his nerves, he took to half a bottle of bourbon each morning before work, a habit he believed to be inconsequential. However, it exacted a toll on his relationships, particularly those of a romantic nature.

He dated a variety of women. None were the type to tie him down, which was for the best. His approach to dating had become a mixture of self-fulfilment and abusive tendencies, followed by self-loathing. He called it a vicious circle and blamed it on the women rather than himself.

There was more success in business, though, which led to lunch and dinner invitations. He heard speeches, met with local dignitaries, and developed a network of peers that broadened his options for new opportunities.

In early 1978, he was to attend the annual Joe Jackson Cancer Foundation Dinner. On this evening, however, he had reached his limit. The thought of another stuffy meal with men in suits discussing profits and market trends, despite being there for a not-for-profit cause, suffocated him.

Steve's formal attire hid his reluctance to be at an upscale restaurant. He fidgeted and struggled to make eye contact with people. The clinking of wine glasses and murmur of small talk filled the air. The night wore on, and his restlessness grew. He excused himself from the table, feigning a headache, and slipped out the side door. The cool air was a welcome relief.

A soft, melodic laugh wafted over from a nearby alley. He followed the intriguing sound, and found himself alone with a woman. A knot tightened in his gut as her short, buxom figure drew him closer, figuratively speaking, of course .

"What are you doing here on your own?" he asked.

"Are you sure you want to listen to those losers? Wouldn't you prefer something or someone genuine? I'm Jane, by the way. Jane Jackson. And you are?"

Jane was the daughter of the wealthiest family in town, and renowned as a free spirit and adventure-seeker. Her stylish chic clashed with thick black leather boots that gave her outfits a delightful unconventionality.

"You look like you could use a break from all that corporate monotony," she said with a mischievous sparkle.

Steve, surprised by her pragmatic sincerity, could only manage a nod of agreement.

Without missing a beat, Jane took his hand and led him away.

What followed was a night of spontaneity and exhilaration. The local jazz club saw them dance until the early hours, after which they drove to a nearby beach. The moonlight reflected off the waves, which lapped upon the shore in sweet unison with their passionate lovemaking.

Jane's vivacious personality and sense of adventure were contagious. She guided Steve through experiences that pushed him out of his comfort zone. They shared stories, dreams, and aspirations under the starlit sky, forging a connection that went beyond the confines of their social backgrounds.

As the night ended, Steve realised he had not only escaped the mundane business dinner, but had also embarked on an unforgettable connection with Jane. It changed everything for him.

Their relationship blossomed and by February the following year, they were engaged. Steve's business interests now had the opportunity to become an empire.

"We can't live here Steve." Jane was used to extravagance and a three-bedroom house would not suffice. "To be honest, I want that big house. You know the one I want. The biggest there is in town."

"That one!" Steve's eyes almost popped out of his skull. "That's massive! Do you think the Allisons will sell?" He remembered the close call, almost getting shot whilst sprinting down the driveway.

"Believe me, he will sell." Her conniving cackle made Steve squirm.

* * *

Jane began turning up at social gatherings she knew the Allisons would attend, and subtly befriended them. Each time, she took her plan to the next step by complimenting their home or encouraging them to discuss preserving its historical integrity. The introduction of her expertise as an architectural planner aided her quest.

All seemed to go well, so after several weeks of coaxing, she was sure they were open to a generous offer.

"We would be happy to take your house to a whole new level and revitalise the entire estate. Plus, we would provide you a handsome compensation. Would you consider $2.5 million a fair offer?"

Jon Allison looked surprised. "We couldn't sell the place! It is our forever home. We intend to keep it in the family for generations. I mean, where else would we go?"

"Come now, Jon. I know there is a price you'd be prepared to sell. What if I said $3 million?"

"Jane, I am sure your intentions are above reproach. Angela and I are getting on in years. We like to say we bought the house for a rock and half a candy bar, and now we want to leave the best possible memories and future for our family. It wouldn't be right to sell. But thanks for the kind offer."

"Thank you, Jon. I do hope your family enjoys many more years in residence." Jane's words sounded so sincere.

She had embedded herself in the upper echelons of local politics and law enforcement. This evolved out of necessity after her father indulged in a late-night shindig with two women, a fair amount of bourbon and the front seat of a Cadillac, with the engine still running.

A fabricated dossier of documents was 'forgotten' on a ledge, but no one appeared to notice. Jane managed, with impeccable skill, to ensure a renowned investigative journalist found it. His enquiries into the documents' contents sparked rumours regarding money laundering through the Allison's businesses.

Jane's walk on part years before on The Andy Griffith Show had made her a local celebrity. She milked the notoriety for all its worth, gaining access to all the best gossips and columnists in town. She was on the phone to Jon as soon as Aunty Ange, the local gossip columnist, gave her the scoop.

"Jon, I don't believe a word of it," Jane said.

"It is all false. This is a conspiracy." Jane sensed Jon words tried to hide his pain. "Why would someone choose to do this to us?"

"Let me see what I can find." Empathy oozed from her every word.

Conversations ensued with a variety of the best gabbers. Each one expressed their concerns and surprise at the news. Jane would say, "It's unfortunate that Jon's business is under such scrutiny." But would follow up later on with, "I'm sure the truth will come out." This led her friends to infer that she knew something but wasn't saying, which fanned the flame into an inferno.

Within a few days, the local paper ran a story and asked Mayor Paul for his view at a news conference.

A day earlier, Jane had been on the phone. "Mayor Paul." Those two words never sat right with Jane. "You need to stop wanting to meet late at night. We agreed to end our affair two months ago."

Jane knew precisely which buttons to push to manipulate him as she desired. "However, I am prepared to make an exception, if you'd like me to." Once in her palm, Mayor Paul listened, and Mayor Paul followed Jane's every word.

Back at the news conference, and looking straight ahead, he said, "Where there is smoke, there is fire." The story remained newsworthy for a couple more days.

"What will you do, Jon?" Jane was keen to show her solidarity with him.

"Nothing." Jane's support had backfired. "It is with friends like you that we can weather this storm. Why would I leave? Don't tell anyone, but the business is suffering. We will see what the next few months brings."

Now armed with inside knowledge, she had the ammunition needed to aim at her target.

Deputy Police Commissioner Howard Jefferson was the youngest of three sons. He was also the youngest to attain Deputy Commissioner in the history of the metropolitan area. His appointment had surprised many, but not the Jackson family. Their surreptitious financial encouragement had ensured glowing endorsements reached the right ears, resulting in repeated swift promotions. The one person well aware of their generosity was Jefferson himself.

Howard was unaware of the ferocity with which Jane would insist he investigate the money laundering. She wanted charges laid in days and gave a clear ultimatum when he asked why. "You are in your position because of my family. If you won't do your job appropriately, we shall have to find someone who will."

Two days later, Jon came into the station for questioning. Attacks in the papers started up again, which had previously tarnished his public image. Now they destroyed it.

After a second round of four hours of questioning, he arrived home shattered, as the phone rang.

"Jon, this is Jane."

"Jane, I can't talk right now, I just…"

"Yes Jon. You can talk right now! All this can disappear."

"I'm listening." Jon said, a scowl protruding across his brow. "What do you have in mind?"

"Your house." A chill ran down Jon's back. "I want your house. I'll give you $2 million."

"You offered $3 million last time!"

"Do you want this to go away? Your choice, Jon."

"Are you going to make this go away? Who are you? God?"

Jane paused. "Don't push me, Jon. You say the word and your legal worries will go on hold until the sale goes through. Once I have the house, the charges will disappear."

Without answers to his problems, Jon gave in to her vice-like grip.

The sale went through in time for Steve and Jane's May wedding, leaving Jon to retire in peace with all charges disappearing.

The wedding itself was a quiet affair. Brian served as best man, one step behind the newlyweds. He had always played second fiddle to their relationship.

Steve had found a strong, domineering figure who would support him despite his failings. Jane was aware of his past anger issues, and didn't forgive him on behalf of past women. Instead, she looked forward; helping him channel it, rather than suppressing his feelings and exploding into rage.

She abided his drinking, however, as she loved her spirits, often savouring a 25-year single malt. Thus, he had episodes that were not pretty, but they usually occurred away from home, so she turned a blind eye.

They were no match made in Heaven, but they complimented one another, and their life together worked for them.

Jane had made it known, however, that her feelings about the two principal men in Steve's life were less amicable. They had always been around, but since the wedding, her patience had worn thin.

Steve's rock was his wife. But anything she might do to oust one or both of them, in the same way she ousted the Allisons, had the potential to make that rock splinter.

FIFTEEN

IT HITS THE FAN

S teve's partner in the car dealership was a self-made success. James Andersen never said no to anyone and always found the good in everyone. If optimism was a sport, he would be on the podium. Well, that's how Steve saw him, anyway.

By 1986, there had been a few tough years for car salesmen, from queuing for hours to buy gas, through to strikes and inflation wreaking havoc with Middle America's personal finances.

The economy had improved, but their books had not, and the bank was on their back. Ways needed to be found to turn things around. James always seemed to have something squirrelled away for a rainy day, confident they would pull through without too big an issue.

Steve wasn't so sure and turned to other means of finance. He would bring back more of his pot of gold from 2023.

He'd been careful in handling the time travel kit and stored it in his personal safe at work. Now was to be the first time he'd used it since 1975.

It was Saturday evening, and Steve was last to leave the office. Everything was in place to travel to 2023 and be back for dinner with

50kg of gold. Everything, except the key for the 2023 safe deposit box. His recollection of what happened to it years earlier was fuzzy. So, once back home, he performed a thorough search.

"Anyone home?" Brian called out as he walked in the front door. "I'm back from Andy's." Jane was out, but Brian found Steve in a frantic state. "What's wrong? You look like you lost something?"

"It's nothing." In his panic to find the key, he'd misplaced both the watch and the device. "Get me a drink."

The night spiralled downhill from there as Steve sank deeper into a sea of booze, consuming far more than his usual substantial intake. "Why did I bring you here? What good is it for me to have my son here from World War Two?" The alcohol revealed truths hidden for years. "I should have left you with your mother! Then none of this would have happened. She wouldn't have died, and I wouldn't have lived with it for the rest of my life!" He slumped back in his chair.

Brian grabbed Steve by the arms. "What do you mean, she died? How did she die?" But in his stupor Steve was asleep. Brian shook his limp body vigorously, but to no effect.

When Sunday morning arrived, before Steve stumbled from his slumber, Jane had already come and gone. She'd seen him in the chair when she arrived home the night before, and left him to snore far from their bedroom, valuing the rare opportunity to sleep well.

Brian found Steve looking likely to vomit, crawling out of the bathroom. He would not address the elephant in the room, knowing that without the booze Steve would avoid the question, plus Brian doubted he could finish a sentence without rushing for the toilet.

There was no longer a safety net for Steve's finances. He would continue to search for the time machines, but they never turned up. In his mind, only one solution existed to drag the business out of its hole, which was to approach past acquaintances. There was always a loan shark around and Steve didn't have to go far to bump into Isaiah; named as such, because one eye was higher than the other.

"It's been a long time, Stevie. What you doing coming here?" They had lost touch over the years, but Isaiah wasn't the same low life Steve had known in a past life. Outside opportunities had come his way and what had been a small-town racket had grown to include connections with a Chicago-based syndicate.

"I need fifty G's. The business is going through a rough patch." Steve could never remember which eye was the glass one, and it made him nervous to offend by looking at the wrong one. "I can pay it back over the next six months."

"Sure, no problem. Leave your first born as collateral." Isaiah raised an eyebrow, revealing the glass eye more clearly.

"You know I'm good for it."

Isaiah laughed. "Of course you are. Why else would I give you a preferential rate?"

The deal was done, and Steve felt vindicated when he brought the money to show James. "No questions asked. Pay off the debts and let's get things moving again."

"I don't know, my friend. When do we have to repay this?"

Steve relaxed in his oversized executive chair. "Don't worry. I've got your back."

They left the conversation there, Steve hoping this would improve their financial position.

Not convinced, James created a plan to protect the business, its integrity, and most of all, himself.

The following week, late on a Friday afternoon, which was always busy with speculators dreaming of upgrading their car, the drinks came out to ease into the big weekend push. Steve would have more than he could handle, and someone would drive him home. This Friday, James made sure it would be him.

They sat across from each other, the weight of the troubled business resting on both their shoulders. James maintained a facade of concern, an act honed over years of negotiations. "Steve," he began, his voice laced with a veneer of sympathy, "I can't help but worry about the company. These financial troubles, they're gnawing at us, eating away at what we've built together."

Steve, nursing a glass of bourbon, looked up, his eyes already clouded, grunted in agreement.

James leaned forward, his face as pale as a prisoner being led to the firing squad. "I've been giving this a lot of thought, Steve. I even sought legal counsel from someone specialising in business restructuring and financial protection."

Steve's eyes peeked over the top of his glasses before setting them on the table. "What did they say?"

James let out a demonstrative sigh. "They were blunt. If we don't act now, things could turn disastrous. Not just for the business, but for us personally. Legal trouble, bankruptcy—the whole nine yards."

Steve's eyes widened as best they could. "What should we do?"

James produced a set of legal documents and slid them across the table. "This is the solution. It's a restructuring plan, one that'll protect both of us and the company. The attorney advised us to implement these changes ASAP. Today, if possible."

Steve glanced at the documents, his brow furrowed as he tried to focus. "What's in there?"

James leaned in once more. "There are certain clauses that will ensure the safeguarding of our interests, especially yours."

Steve hesitated, his fingers tracing the edges of the papers. "And what about you?"

James shook his head slowly. "I've poured my life into this

business. I can't bear to see it crumble. But more than that, I don't want to see you go down with it. We're partners, Steve, in every sense of the word."

A pang of guilt washed over Steve. He'd brought this financial turmoil into their lives, and now, it seemed, James was the only one offering a long-term lifeline. "But what's in it for you, James?"

James leaned back, his eyes locking onto Steve's. "I'll be honest. This restructuring has provisions that protect my personal assets. It's a necessary precaution, but it benefits both of us."

With a heavy sense of urgency, Steve's emotions wavered between guilt, gratitude, and a creeping sense of desperation.

James, his gaze never wavering, added, "Time is against us, Steve. I've put my trust in you, and in us. Let's sign these papers and move forward with our future."

Steve's gut-feeling had served him well in life. Without total assurance either way, it told him James was right, and he played his hand. He fingered through the documents, under the pretence of reading one last section. "I trust you, man. Where do I sign?"

They shook on the deal and the dye was cast, but the consequences were yet to unfold.

The first tremor of this seismic shift arrived a month after the ink had dried on those fateful papers, when the loan's initial repayment came due. James, out of town and unavailable, left Steve to grapple with it on his own. As he delved into the financial statements, a growing sense of unease gnawed at him. The numbers stared back, diminished from their previous state. Confusion twisted his features as he demanded answers from Scott, their financial controller.

"What's happened to our cash flow? These numbers are way down in the last few months," Steve asked, his tone laced with a mounting sense of dread.

Scott, unruffled but still burdened with the truth, replied, "Mr. Harding, that would be because of the restructure you agreed with James." On James' orders, he'd implemented the changes before Steve understood the true impact.

Steve's complexion paled, the gravity of the situation hitting home like a ton of bricks. "How do you mean?" he asked.

Scott chose his words. "Well," he began, "you own half the business, and James owns the rest. But you don't own the same assets anymore. Or, to be more precise, you own two separate businesses."

The words hung in the air, and for a moment Steve's world seemed to crumble around him. He leapt from his chair, a fiery determination in his eyes, and headed straight for Scott, who beat a hasty retreat from the impending storm, leaving Steve to handle his newfound reality in solitude.

He scrutinised the documents, gaining a deeper understanding of their implications, which turned his stomach. The car lots, once owned equally, were now split. James now owned the lion's share of the most profitable ones, while Steve retained the burden of the least profitable and the loss-makers. The magnitude of James' betrayal and cunning manipulation hit Steve like a frying pan to the face.

"I'm gonna kill him!" Steve's furious proclamation reverberated through the office, silencing everyone within earshot.

Five minutes later, after a wild phone conversation with a riled-up Steve, Jane's reaction was like a tempest unleashed upon everything close by, leaving a trail of destruction in her wake.

"Don't worry," her voice rang down the line, oozing authority and conviction. "He will pay most dearly." Steve knew he needn't worry about seeking vengeance. His imagination was but a drop in an ocean of unimaginable cruelty that Jane could conjure up.

After the initial shock, he paid off the looming debt by diverting funds from other business interests. And so, life for Steve settled into an uneasy equilibrium once more in this thief to riches story.

His unease remained, as isolation enveloped him, brought on by still keeping his one truly shameful episode a secret. The time had arrived, though, to confide in the only person he trusted intimately.

Jane had banished Brian from the house after a tense argument, caused by jealousies about who Steve favoured more. Steve arrived home after preparing to go away on a last-minute business trip the next day. Jane was collecting herself, which, for Steve, meant she was calming down after becoming flustered about something. She would need his sympathy prior to the unburdening of his yoke.

"Is there something wrong?" Steve was afraid of the potential response.

"It's that boy!" Her scowl reflected the hatred she'd developed for Brian. "Your nephew needs to go."

"Oh Jane, I'm sorry." His hand held hers, as they both knew this was not their typical chat. "I love you, but I love him too."

"You used the L word twice in a sentence, and one was about someone else." Jane's face changed to one of surprise. "You haven't used it twice in two years when talking about me!"

"Listen." Steve's eyes dropped to the floor. "It's time you know everything."

"I'm listening." With a look of concern, Jane turned and waited.

"He's not my nephew and his name isn't Brian."

"He's yours, isn't he?" The scowl returned.

"Yes. And his name is Joe."

"And what came of the mother? Did she abandon him?" Jane stood as tall as her frame allowed and looked down upon Steve, who had slumped to the ground.

"I killed her." His head bowed before tears flowed.

The dark reality hit Jane full in the face. She paused before handing out orders for Steve to follow. "Get up and stop the self-pity. I'm sure she deserved it. Your life goes on, and that's what matters now."

Steve knew his wife to be strong-willed, but this went to a whole different level, and his tears turned off almost instantly, out of shock.

The following day, Steve left for Florida to deal with a supplier, leaving Brian, who hadn't come home that night, to deal with Jane. Steve knew him to be a resourceful soul and trusted that he'd be fine. Little did he know, though, he was never to see Brian again.

* * *

Evening came and Jane attended a meeting in the town hall. She made herself conspicuous, as this was to be her alibi for what she had planned. A couple of out-of-town heavies were to hang around James Andersen's favourite haunt from 7pm that Saturday evening, the sports bar where the wings were even more divine than the women (James' words, not Jane's). After following him home, they were to beat him within an inch of his life, ensuring he was conscious when they left.

The meeting finished and all Jane could wonder was whether she had spent her money wisely. Whilst still half a mile from home, her taxi hardly moved. "There must be an accident, ma'am."

However, as they approached her front gates, a serious commotion involving police had Jane concerned. She paid the driver before approaching an officer. "What's happening? This is my house."

"Can you come this way please, ma'am?" The officer directed her to a mobile police unit to speak with his captain.

The captain spoke in a simple, clear tone. "Mrs Harding?"

"Yes, captain. You must be new here. I haven't seen you before."

"I am ma'am. Do you know James Andersen?"

An air of foreboding drifted over Jane. "Yes, he is a business partner of my husband's."

"Do you know why he would have been at your house this evening?"

"What? No. I have no idea whatsoever. What's this all about? Why can't I get access to my house?"

"I'm afraid someone murdered Mr Andersen in your house tonight, ma'am." Jane stumbled, struggling to remain upright. The captain turned to his officer and motioned for her to provide assistance.

"No. No. I'll be alright. I'll stay at a hotel for the night." She flagged down the same taxi. The driver hadn't left, rapt by the show of flashing police lights and TV cameras.

In her hotel room, Jane lay on the bed in horror. She had no way of contacting her heavies, as they were not able to identify each other. For once, she felt shocked at what she had done.

It was several days before the police allowed Steve and Jane into the house, having completed their onsite investigations. Police questioned them both, but suspicion fell on their nephew Brian, the only person seen running from the house after gunshots rang out through the neighbourhood.

In the midst of her guilt, Jane encouraged the Brian theory, and the investigation remained open. However, no one ever saw Brian again.

SIXTEEN

A MOTHER'S SON

Joe never considered himself to be Brian. From the day he arrived in 1975, his final thought before falling asleep kept his identity and his mother's memory alive.

He played it safe with Jane, avoiding both physical and emotional connection. By 1986, an ever-growing tension had built, which spilt over into an all-out verbal fight.

Before this, however, Joe questioned Steve's credentials as his father. Not whether he was his biological son, but because of the way he'd ended up in 1980s America, whether Steve had his best interests at heart. He failed to understand why Steve hid the time machines from him and never mentioned their travels through time. So, when the opportunity came to take possession of the devices, he grabbed it.

Steve had instinctively handed Joe the key to his safe deposit box the day they arrived in 1975. In his frustration, however, whilst hiding the gold, he forgot to retrieve it. Joe never brought up the subject, but protected the velvet bag with the key inside.

Joe was aware of the financial woes the car business was going through. How could he fail to, when Steve was often shouting about it during one of his drunken stupors? He knew it would be a matter of time before he would try to bring back more gold, which would mean searching for the key.

The day Steve arrived home to find the key, Joe was already there. The place was so large that you could spend hours walking around and see no one.

Steve came home on this occasion, didn't see Joe, but Joe had noticed how frustrated he seemed. All his muttering to himself was typical. With the time machines sitting on a cupboard, and Steve scrunched underneath looking in the deepest darkest corner, Joe swiped them, walked outside, and pretended to have just arrived back from his friend Andy's.

He wasn't yet ready to use them, though. Instead, a burning desire to learn the truth about his mother's fate consumed him.

Resolution came on the evening of 29th July 1986, the night after his fight with Jane.

He had wanted to revisit an episode in his own life from several years prior. Back To The Future was playing at the cinema. At the last moment, he bought a ticket and sat as close to the exit as possible. Aware the credits were about to roll, he left and walked to a shadowy doorway to watch the impending show. Joe watched, mesmerised, as a memory unfolded before him. He cried for the young boy he saw running and disappearing with a flash of light. But when two chasers appeared, one of which he remembered to be John, he had no desire to start up a conversation about temporal coincidences. Instead, he turned to run home.

He only made it a few metres, though, before John approached from in front of him. Joe was gobsmacked that John could move so fast and change clothes. But this was the same John that he knew from his childhood in Liverpool. So, when he asked, "Brian? Is that you?"

Joe didn't know what to say at first.

He slowed to a jog, realising John didn't recognise him as Joe, but stopped and stared straight at him. It struck Joe that the man staring back had no concept of him as a man. He remembered how, during her last couple of days alive, his mother was happy with John around, and, with longing in his voice, said, "If only." With that, he darted past John, not prepared to discuss Brian or Joe or anything else.

The emotional experience of seeing himself and coming across Jane in one of her stubborn moods, caused Joe to snap. He did not hold back from telling Jane everything he'd held inside for years, before leaving the house. However, he stayed on the property.

No one else was aware of his presence, as Jane and Steve got drunk and Steve revealed the truth about Joe and his mother. Joe overheard it all, implanting the last piece of the puzzle he needed to leave this life behind. A deep hatred for Steve germinated in his heart that day.

Unbeknown to Steve and Jane, Joe had built a bond with James Andersen that was healthier than the bond he had with Steve. It was what Joe thought a proper uncle and nephew relationship should be like. After hearing his father's confession, Joe asked James if he could stay the night at his place. James agreed with no need for an explanation.

"Can we put Revolver on?" Joe asked, for his one link back to Liverpool was his love for The Beatles, cultivated by memorable evenings spent chilling with James. Had they been aware of what the following day held, they might have pushed through the drowsiness and indulged in deeper conversation, combined with more cool tunes. But as it was, the psychedelic tones of Tomorrow Never Knows faded, and they called it a night. They never discussed Joe's overheard conversation.

The new day began with such promise. Joe relished spending one final day with James, who was as optimistic as ever, with a healthy business and supportive family.

It was a Wednesday morning, which James always began with a jog; nothing strenuous, just a couple of miles. Joe agreed to join him, and being early on a summer's day, there were plenty of other joggers about. Soon after turning back, a tall stranger joined them. By the way he spoke, Joe was sure he was from out of town.

"How do y'all find running in this heat? Surviving?" He was friendly enough, and they chatted.

His intention seemed geared towards getting acquainted with locals, asking where they were from and if they had family in town. A shy Joe, uncomfortable with such impinging on their privacy, glanced at James, who chatted away with complete openness. "We've been living here for some time now. My boy Brian is here for company today."

The casual remark rendered a nod from the jogger. "That's nice, bonding while exercising."

Joe tried to make a point. "It was until…"

The jogger didn't let him finish, and butted in saying, "Oh, Uncle, you say." His speech slowed. "You look like father and son."

Without showing much interest, James agreed, "Great way to start the day."

To the surprise of his acquaintances, as quickly as he'd arrived, he left. "I'm off down here. See you again." The brief episode seemed a little odd to Joe, but James didn't look concerned.

Later that afternoon, however, Joe was all prepared to bid farewell, having one final outing to complete. Dressed in his favourite hoodie and jeans, he almost walked straight into the same jogger guy. "Where are you off to in such a rush?"; his snappy dress-sense surprising Joe.

"Oh, hello!" Joe peered back. "Isn't this a coincidence?"

"Brian, isn't it?" There was a knowing glint in his eye.

"Hang on! I never told you me name." Joe's former scouse accent sneaked out. "Who told yer that?" His head turned, looking to see if anyone was watching. "What you after, mister?"

"Hey, calm down, man. My friend over there," pointing at Isaiah across the street, "said where I find you, I'll find your uncle. I want to talk with him."

"Who told you that? Isaiah?"

"You know him?" the man asked.

"Everyone knows him around here."

Isaiah watched as they kept pointing in his direction.

"What's his real name?"

"I dunno." Joe walked away. "I'm off. I don't know or care where my uncle is."

Joe continued on to meet James at his usual Wednesday night bar. Joe was on the hard stuff, milk, and James drank his usual Bud. They discussed the overheard conversation, and Joe got upset.

"Listen." James put an arm round Joe. "Let's get outta here. It's better if we talk somewhere quieter."

He opted to go home, but Joe paused. "I need to get something from my place first. I'll only be a few minutes."

Within ten minutes, they both hung a left and drove up to the house. "Good. No one's home." The relief was obvious on Joe's face. "I refuse to talk with either of them ever again."

"Why are we here?" James tried to grab Joe's arm to get his attention.

"I'm not staying. I'm leaving town tonight, and I won't be returning." Joe tried to allay the concern he saw on James' face.

"You're what?" James stopped dead in his tracks. Joe carried on walking and entered the house, so James had no choice but to follow. "Why are you leaving?" No matter how much James tried to get Joe to stop, Joe kept walking, continuing into the ballroom.

"James, I don't want to be around those two ever again. I have something I need to do, and I can't do it here." Joe turned and started towards his reason for the diversion: to collect the time machine.

"Why? What is so urgent that you must leave right away?" Desperation was not a part of James' usual persona, but despite having a son of his own, the young man he knew as Brian was akin to a second son. "Whatever it is, let me help you."

"James, stop!" Joe meant stop talking, but reality can be cruel. The sound of someone fumbling with metal on metal distracted Joe, his gaze turning towards the doorway. Confused that anyone else would even be in the house, he strained to see who it was, but James blocked his view.

James didn't appear concerned, swivelling clockwise on the heel of his right shoe. The power of a single bullet then ripped through his body, pushing him backwards towards Joe, and collapsing at his feet.

A moment later, Joe fell backwards, as something slammed into the centre of his chest. His breathing became short and shallow, and Joe turned his head downwards in fear he'd been shot.

There was a hole in his shirt, but the blood he expected didn't appear. Buttons scattered across the floor as he ripped the shirt open. St Christopher hung in front of his breastbone, warped and unrecognisable, the bullet still lodged in it. A sudden pang of unsteady queasiness nearly saw him black out.

Instead, he managed to pull himself together, and with helpless abandon, screwed the consequences and unfurled his anger. "What the hell are you doing here?" he screamed at the shooter. "Why would you kill someone you don't know? You jogged with us this morning!"

The response was cold. "Your uncle owed my uncle." The words that followed shook Joe to his core. "I've been hunting him for years, and now I can finally put this baby to bed."

"You moron! This isn't my uncle!" The incredulity in Joe's voice strained with pain as he realised James was not the intended target.

"Yeah, right! We arm-wrestled a few years back. This is him."

"You shot me as well!"

"Yeah. I meant to hit him. My bad." With that, the man with no name tossed the gun across the room, turned, and walked out of the house, disappearing into the night.

Joe had already stopped listening, and only semi-noticed the man's actions as he'd scrambled to his knees, maintaining steady pressure on the gaping wound to stem the flow of blood pouring from James.

"Stay with me, James!" Joe's eyes welled up, his hands overwhelmed with incessant redness.

Within seconds, James' breathing weakened. Joe pressed two fingers against his neck, searching for a pulse. However, only a few seconds later, he experienced James' transition from life to death. He nestled James' head into his lap and sobbed.

Thoughts that descended into a dark dominion of despair overwhelmed him. "Where do I go from here? My life may as well end along with James. I can't bear another painful loss like this." He mulled the pros and cons over in his mind for ending it all.

It was while soul searching that an awareness of the deep pain in his chest increased. Joe was not religious, but with his head raised, he thanked his mother for protecting him. Memories of her joy for life and strength of character flooded back, reminding him how to find the good in, and squeeze the juicy bits from, a sometimes-bitter existence. His mindset switched from the notion of suicide to the hope of a life worth living.

By the time he'd made his mind up, though, James' blood was all over him. He retrieved the time travel devices, but decided there was one other item he wanted. Uncertain where it was, he ripped the room apart, overturning tables and tearing art from the walls in desperation. It took a few minutes, but his efforts seemed worth it, once he possessed the murder weapon.

Not wanting to leave a trail of blood in his car, he ran to James' place, darting around and avoiding streetlights, hoping to remain unseen. There, he showered and changed before making a sandwich. Joe's journey to the distant future, in a distant land, was about to end.

Five minutes later, he was back in 1941 Liverpool as a man. No longer was he the little boy that his father could manipulate. On the contrary, he intended to manipulate his father, as his focus turned to preventing his mother's murder.

SEVENTEEN

BATTLE AGAINST TIME

Monday 5th May 1941, 11.00am, Liverpool

Joe's boyhood memories of leaving 1941 were not as sharp as he'd hoped. He remembered where he lived, but the precise date they'd left was fuzzy. As such, he arrived the morning after he'd left, appearing from thin air right in the middle of central Liverpool, wearing a mullet, jeans and Bon Jovi T-shirt. One woman freaked out so much she had to be revived after fainting. Others wanted to lynch him, as the sudden materialising from nowhere had people believing this was some kind of Nazi infiltration. It made no difference, remonstrating with them in his native scouse. All he could do was run.

The crowd were in two minds whether he was a Nazi, but some decided he must be. Three servicemen in their civvies weren't about to let him escape; pursuing Joe, who already had a thirty-metre head start. But Joe's weakness at running meant he relied more on wit and luck than speed.

A minute in, and an air-raid siren sounded. Joe bolted into a shop, searching for an exit out the back. He wasn't about to follow the rules, but hoped that the big burly army guys would. Two chose to avoid a court martial, but the one remaining couldn't give a rat's fart what the army might do to him, and knowing the area well, guessed Joe would run through the shop, so lay in wait around the back.

Joe rushed out, his senses alert to anyone following.

"Hello Darling!" Smack! The fist hit him high on the back of the head. "Where you think you're going, Fritz?"

Joe stumbled, but stayed on his feet. More stunned at being found than by the punch, he tried once more to explain himself.

Smack! A left hook hit hard. That one hurt, getting it right on the bridge of the nose.

"OK," he said under his breath. "Fight Time." The old schoolboy days with a friend called Tank came back to him.

Another blow rained in, which he sidestepped to his right and countered with a right to the guy's windpipe.

The soldier withdrew, spluttering for air, trying to regain his composure. But Joe was taking no chances. With hands on the guy's shoulders, his knee slammed into the nuts. Bent over in pain, there was no protection for when Joe used his knee again to smash his adversary's nose. Blood splattered and poured from the fractured nasal passages. Joe turned and fled.

There were still a few minutes to escape to safety, and once he was a fair distance from the altercation, asked for help to find a shelter.

The musty concrete bunker, filled with chatter and all sorts of odours, reverted Joe to his childhood in an instant. He drew comfort from the nostalgia that his mother was always close by. It was difficult to go with the flow now, though. The cramped conditions and constant noise were foreign to how life had been these past eleven years. However, there was no choice, and he'd have to wait it out.

Five hours passed and the all-clear sounded. To walk out from the shelter and breathe fresh air again was like being freed from a tomb and he was ready to find his old home.

It was a bit of a trek, but despite the drizzly rain he was upbeat as memories flooded back. At the main road, a hundred metres before their street, his mood became sombre and introspective. As he turned the corner, anticipating a return to his childhood home thrilled him with excitement. Once around the corner, though, the reality broke his heart. The house was gone. In fact, half the houses on the street were gone, including Mrs Evans' place next door. Fires burned and bricks were strewn everywhere.

Joe's mind raced to understand the implications. He'd arrived some time after his previous departure. But how long after?

He had to know and so knocked on one of the remaining houses. "Hello. I don't mean to be a nuisance or anything, but when did those houses get bombed?"

"Last night." The neighbour shook his head. "I heard it coming, like. It was so close I thought it would defo hit us."

"Last night?" Joe had an idea. "Did anyone die in a house in the neighbourhood recently?"

"They're all dead now, aren't they?"

"Sorry, I mean, other than caused by the bombing."

"No! Why do you ask?"

"You know Joyce Tuttle, don't you?" Without wanting to let on that he knew Mr Todd, who stood at the door, Joe pushed to get answers.

"Yeah, of course I do." Mr Todd pointed down the road. "She lived at number seventeen."

"Lived at? Why do you say lived at? Did something happen to her?"

Mr Todd's eyes narrowed and with a subtle shake of the head, he said, "Because there ain't no house at number seventeen anymore, is there? I only saw her yesterday as well. She and some fancy older gent." Mr Todd turned to ask a question, but Joe's head was down. He was walking away. "Where you going? Did I say something wrong?"

All evidence of Joyce's murder, and even her very existence, had gone forever. Hatred had built towards Steve, and Joe was now plotting how he would travel back one day and stop him.

He stopped and returned to Mr Todd. "Do you have a gun or a knife or something?" Joe was over niceties and manners.

"I don't know you. And why would I have a gun? I'm not a soldier." Mr Todd started to close the door, but Joe's foot blocked it. "Sorry. Nah! Get me the biggest knife you have. You have one minute."

Mr Todd wasn't up for a fight, so Joe was out of there with a knife and heading for a back alley. Once alone, he travelled back twenty-four hours.

Monday 4th May 1941, 7.04pm, Liverpool

"You have got to be kidding me!" Joe searched everywhere for the knife, patting down his pockets and looking all around.

Amid his panic, he heard footsteps passing the alley. He saw them, but they didn't see him. It was Joyce, John, and Joe, returning home. Joe, transfixed by his mother, welled up. His mouth opened to call out but stopped short of making a sound.

Unseen, he watched them walk the rest of the way, tears now streaming down his face. After several minutes, he regained his composure and realised the knife had not come with him. There was no way he could barge into the Todd household again and get the knife either. He wanted to find what had happened to it. A quick journey to a little under twenty-four hours ahead, showed him what had occurred.

Monday 5th May 1941, 6.54pm, Liverpool

Joe hid from himself inside an empty trash can fifteen metres down the alley and waited. After what seemed like an hour later, his earlier self came running round the corner with the knife in his left hand. With the time machine set, he gave it a shake. There was the flash of light and the knife fell to the ground as he disappeared.

Joe was all set to return to yesterday and picked up the knife, this time in his right hand, and gave the device a shake.

Monday 4th May 1941, 6.34pm, Liverpool

"Argh!! Where's it gone now?" There had to be some explanation why the knife failed to travel, but Joe would not waste time finding out.

"I'm in the middle of a war. There must be a weapon I can find here." He wracked his brain for ideas. There was a scrap heap half a mile away. He only needed something like a solid pipe. Joe searched for anything hard that he could hit Steve with. The only things available were bits of old broken wood and they were only large enough to give someone a splinter. "I know. I'll confront him before he gets to Mum and that interference should disrupt history to prevent him from killing her."

Joe didn't believe Steve was hiding inside the house when they arrived home, so must have arrived after dinner. He watched John leave to go next door and took up a position two doors down. It wasn't long before things stirred, except it was not who he expected.

"Eh! I remember you!" Joe heard a voice, but wasn't sure where it came from. "You're that Nazi. Don't you move!" He noticed a face at a neighbour's window disappear and the front door open. "Bill, come on. Let's get him."

Joe paused for a second, poised ready to take on the two men running at him. Soon enough, though, that seemed foolish, and he turned and sprinted away as best he could. There was an escape route he knew from childhood days that took him through two backyards and over a shed roof. He'd never found it to be as useful as he did on that occasion. On his belly under a hedgerow, the two pursuers ran past and, having lost the trail, Joe heard them decide to return to their friend's house.

"OK, I need a new plan, " he thought. He knew Steve turned up around ten o'clock, so Joe could do nothing yet. It was time to travel once more.

Monday 4th May 1941, 9.44pm, Liverpool

Back in the alley, Joe emerged onto the street and walked in the direction Steve would come from. He found a secluded spot and waited once more. Only one more minute and he expected to see Steve come walking by.

Two minutes passed. No sign of Steve. Another two minutes. Nothing. "Where could he be?" Joe's mind whirled in disbelief. He waited a few minutes longer before deciding to return to his street and see if anything was happening.

By the time he turned the corner, he could see John running out of the house and into next door. A couple of minutes later, John ran into Josey's house. "That must have been after I left. Mum's already dead." Joe's mumblings helped keep his thoughts clear. "It's like some invisible force is preventing me from saving Mum. What is this? The rules of time travel or something! Thou shalt not save a person's life. Stuff the time travel gods. I don't care. I'm gonna save her!"

No sooner had those words echoed to the heavens than the air-raid siren began. An elderly neighbour from three doors down walked by on his way home. "I wouldn't go home tonight, Mr North."

"I'll be fine, son. My home is my castle." He continued on his way.

"Believe me, please. I know what's about to happen." But Mr North was out of range. His hearing only worked within a five-metre radius.

There was nothing more Joe could do for his mum without travelling back again, but he'd lost count of how many of him were there now, floating around at different times. And would there be some sort of paradox if he were to run into himself? "Only one way to find out," he thought, and the plan to beat all plans was born.

Monday 4th May 1941, 9.43pm, Liverpool

Back in the alley, Joe waited for someone completely different. He awaited himself.

A minute later, Joe walked by and heard, "Joe!"

The newly appeared Joe turned and saw himself, waiting in the alley. "Aargh! Is this allowed?"

"Only one way to find out. Come here. Give us a hug!" Joe came from the alley, inching closer and closer to the other.

"Are you sure this is a good idea?" The new Joe inched backwards.

"No idea, but I've tried everything to save mum and failed. I reckon I can do this if there is an army of us. So, come over here, you big baby, and let's either save Mum or melt the universe down into paradoxical oblivion."

"Hmmm. Great idea. How did I ever come up with this masterpiece?" The new Joe inched forward. "Oh boy! This is going to get real weird, real fast!" They closed their eyes and gave each other a loose man-hug.

"Ew! You stink!"

"Speak for yourself!" The original Joe took a proper look at his other self. "Have you seen how unkempt you look?"

"Yeah, I'm just finding out," said the other.

"Your, I mean, my hair and beard have grown loads more than usual. All this constant time warp stuff must have affected our body or maybe aged us, or something." They released their hug, and life continued without a major universal meltdown.

The Joe who devised the plan called himself Number One and the other guy Number Two.

"I may stink, but that's no reason to call me number two! "

"Are you OK with being Number Three instead?"

Number Three waited until 10.30pm before returning to 9.43pm, a minute before he had last appeared. They named him Number Four, even though there were now three of them. At 10.29pm he travelled back to 9.42pm. And so the loop continued as each subsequent Joe waited until a minute before the previous one travelled back, and they would travel to one minute before their predecessor arrived. One by one they created an army of Joes, all being present in a single timeline.

As the tenth version of himself appeared, they figured that would suffice.

Monday 4th May 1941, 9.35pm, Liverpool

The last Joe appeared in the alley, and they were all together, but no one embraced, having been uncomfortable when they tried that earlier. The idea of too many chefs spoiling the broth came to mind, but they needed a leader. Although they all devised the plan, Number One took his Bon Jovi shirt off to make it easy to identify him as the leader of the pack.

An army of ten walked down to within ten houses of their place and waited. The one thing they didn't want was for their mother to be alerted to their presence, so maintained a safe distance.

Soon after, the two guys from the house over the street came out.

The sight of so many Joes freaked them out, and they ran.

"Yeah, losers!" shouted ten voices in unison, all making the same two-finger salute.

Confidence grew amongst the group, and they waited for Steve, who they expected any minute. They waited, and they waited, but Steve never came.

"Hey," said Number Seven, "that guy just disappeared!"

"Who?" Number Three turned to see.

"One of us," said Number Seven. "It must have been Number One."

"Are you sure?" Number Five looked around. "How many of us are there now?"

They all counted each other. "Nine."

"Agh!" Eight of them let out the same yell as another disappeared.

A minute later, another was gone, and sixty seconds later, yet another.

Number Nine grabbed hold of Number Six and shook him. "What the hell is happening?"

"I don't ..." Number Six vanished.

Those remaining guessed that somehow, each was returning to the alley in some sort of temporal loop, but had no way to prevent their dwindling number.

A little before 10.30pm, Numbers Ten and Eleven remained. "Guess I'm next," said Number Ten.

"OK, see you." And then there was one. The last to arrive was the only Joe left.

"Ah crap!" Talking to himself helped ease the stress. "If Steve turns up now, how am I going to stop him by myself?"

He approached the house from a distance, saw John run inside and soon afterwards run out again, leaving the front door open. Joe knew this was his opportunity to discover for himself what lay inside.

Full of trepidation, he entered, walking through the downstairs rooms. Nostalgia overwhelmed him, but the anticipation of his mother's body close by, eradicated the memories.

The sight of his beloved mother, savaged and lifeless, struck Joe's heart, mind, and soul beyond anything he'd imagined. Unable to bring himself to touch her, he turned and ran, and kept running, only stopping to shelter from falling bombs. Nothing had prepared him for the emotional disaster he experienced that night. The psychological horror devastated him to the core, preventing him from ever attempting to save her again.

He saw her but failed to say goodbye, which lay within his soul like curdled milk on an empty stomach. Depression grew in every element of his being and life became less about survival and more of an existence. The park benches and overpasses of Liverpool were home, as he dodged the draft and spiralled downward into a hellish procession of violence and booze.

The months passed, and whilst rummaging through a bin and numbed by the cold November rain, he searched for any morsel to ease his incessant hunger. A half-eaten piece of pie was the solitary meal that day. In an instant, his mind was in his childhood home. Feelings about his mother flooded back that had remained dormant for six months, and in his mind, he revisited a happier moment in her life.

In the depths of despair, he did more than just remember. He travelled back in person to see that moment one last time. Out came the devices, and Joe returned to that familiar alley a day before her demise.

From the shadows across the street, he watched John walk her home. Her laugh and body language showed such delight, as they chatted like school kids. The power of her happiness broke something inside Joe, and a tear slipped out. The idea was to remain unnoticed, but as he wiped away more tears, he hadn't realised that John was walking towards his location.

"Brian? Is that you?"

Joe wanted one more look to see his mother, but she was already inside the house. With John coming too close for comfort, he fled into the night.

His lasting memory of Joyce had transformed into one of true happiness, which settled something inside, and life could move forward. Joe's hope emanated from his mother once again.

Life did indeed move forward. The time machine came in handy to clean himself up, after which he joined the Royal Navy, serving his country alongside many other brave individuals. As The War ended, he married and life hit all the right notes. He had a family once more. The marriage lasted twenty years, and as often happens, when one door closes, another opens.

At another of life's crossroads, he visited an American town he knew well from a different era. The year was 1965 and opportunities for Brits in towns across America were few, but he persisted and took a job as a welder.

Several years later, he noticed a local news article about a time capsule being entombed on Sunday 24th June 1973 and due to be opened fifty years to the day in 2023. "I've been there," he thought, and an inkling of an idea germinated.

Joe realised his name would be linked with James' murder in 1986. With that being in the future, and knowing the truth, he could clear his name, although nothing would happen before 2023.

There were a couple of issues. First, and most importantly, what to put inside the capsule that would convince authorities of his innocence? Second, how to get anything into the capsule? There was no free for all with kids donating their Jackson Five album or Donny Osmond poster. There was a local competition, though, for one item to be included that people voted for.

Joe was not a dishonest person, but in his fifty-three years, he had picked up a few cunning techniques that might come in handy to manipulate the competition and benefit his cause. None of that knowledge became necessary, though.

Instead, during his few months down and out in Liverpool, he'd learnt to break and enter premises with ease.. The night before the time capsule was to be sealed, he broke into the container holding the items. He swapped out an item with one of his own, sealed it inside a metal box, and no one would be any the wiser.

The next day, the local school was ready with two hundred visitors watching each object enter the capsule one by one. Joe's went in first, resting on the bottom. As far as everyone knew, it was a fruitcake, the kind someone makes for a wedding that lasts for years. That's what the label said, anyway.

After being sealed, they lowered it into a watertight concrete hole. An inscription described the treasure below and the date it was to be opened. The crowd dispersed, leaving workmen to seal a monument in place, covering the hole.

A solitary figure on a hill observed the proceedings from afar, leaned up against an old oak tree. He walked away, kicking a stone in carefree bliss, his legs bowed slightly.

EIGHTEEN

JOHN'S RETURN

In a heartbeat, John traversed the temporal expanse, transitioning from 1986 to the realm of the 21st century. With an ardent curiosity, he yearned to gauge the extent to which recent events had reshaped the tapestry of his remembered reality. Back in Hometown, he retraced his own footsteps and schedule, whilst safeguarding against any inadvertent crossing of paths. An interaction could, he thought, convolute time's delicate threads because of the paradoxical nature of such an occurrence.

John's home coming commenced within the sheltered expanse of woods on the opposite end of the school from where he knew he'd previously been at that moment. The school's buzz of activity reached his ears. So, draped in a hoodie, he resolved to integrate himself into the gathering crowd, and participate in the unfolding excitement.

Like before, a throng of people had congregated around a capsule positioned at the periphery of the schoolyard. John squeezed his way close to the front as dignitaries engaged in removing the capsule from its vault. When it emerged, the mayor picked up the microphone, hushed the crowd and read the inscription aloud.

"His Honor the Mayor, Peter Lansbury, sealed this capsule as a record of life in Hometown on Sunday June 24th, 1973. To be opened by Hometown's mayor in the presence of our people on Saturday June 24th, 2023."

Inside, on top of all the items, was an inventory detailing the capsule's contents. The first item removed was a student's school science book, which stood up well to fifty years of vacuum-packed bliss. Written in bold writing on the front was the name Kevin Johnson. As the mayor leant in to pull out the next item, an elderly gentleman shouted from the crowd, "Can I have it back? I want it back. That's my book. I'm Kevin Johnson, and I've been looking for that for fifty years." The crowd hushed and the mayor's discomfort was obvious, but he replied, "Come and get it, old timer." Kevin climbed onto the stage and held the book aloft as though he'd won a trophy. The crowd cheered, and the mayor muttered something under his breath, which must have been rude, for Kevin gave him a dirty look and returned to join the masses.

One by one, items came out. People oohed aahed and applauded. The final item was a box labelled "Jane Harding's Sumptuous Fruitcake".

The mayor turned to a short, elderly lady on stage, and asked, "Jane, would you do the honours?"

She hobbled over, before turning back to beckon to someone offstage to join.

From no more than ten metres away, John watched as he recognised the face of the much older figure of a man that slowly walked with a limp to join his wife. John couldn't help himself. "What the…!" blurted out more clearly than he'd hoped, as those around gave him strange looks. His mind raced wondering how Steve Harding was no longer just a memory in the annals of Hometown history. "Isn't he dead? Crap! It's not a butterfly effect. But man, that's huge!"

"Will you stop talking!" The old lady to his left gave him a shove.

Onstage, with a broad smile, Jane opened the box. But there was no cake. Inside was a note beside a dark stained handkerchief.

Compelled to read the note aloud, the mayor took it from her.

"In June 1986, someone murdered James Andersen, a much-loved member of this community. I was with James when he died. I did not kill him, but I saw the man shoot him. This gun killed James." He looked back into the box at the handkerchief and, using a couple of pens, tried to pick it up. As he lifted the cloth, a Glock-17 pistol fell to the floor, and a loud gasp came from those close by.

The mayor turned back to the note. Total silence encouraged him to continue in a loud, clear voice.

"Match the gun to its owner and you'll have your killer. This gun belongs to Steve Harding." The mayor's voice softened and slowed. "Steve Harding killed James Andersen. Your 2023 technologies will match the bullet to his gun. Signed: Brian Harding."

A look of total shock overcame the mayor as his face turned pale. He turned to look in the direction of Steve, before placing the letter and other evidence back in the box and closing it.

Police officers came up on stage and managed the box as a piece of evidence. The sergeant wore latex gloves to open the box. "What's this on the back?" he said, having turned the note over.

P.S. Whoever stole my time machines yesterday, please give them back. It wasn't funny that you swapped them for a rock and half a candy bar.

He turned to find Steve, both to his left and then his right, looking everywhere. But Steve was nowhere to be seen, as was Jane.

The crowd soon wandered off, as a solitary figure leaned against an old oak tree from a vantage point on a hill, having observed from a distance. He turned, walked away, and with a flash of light, vanished.

John didn't move. He had hoped to maintain a low profile as a precaution, but the mind-blowing changes and revelations he'd just witnessed left him standing alone, pondering everything. He considered Brian to have been some clever cookie, but getting that letter into the capsule was genius.

He had already noticed that his other self had driven away, so it was safe to make his way home via some detours. It wouldn't be until late evening that his time travel excursions would begin, so he hung around town, waiting for the house to be empty.

Top of mind was to check out the safe deposit box. So, after buying a briefcase and a wallet, John strolled into The First National Bank. The clerk asked for a signature and the key. He withdrew the key from where he'd secured it against his body. She commented they had wondered if anyone would ever show up to claim that box, to which John replied with a wry smile, "Funny. It feels like I was in here just this morning, opening the account."

Once the money was in the briefcase, he waited in line before asking at the teller's window to deposit $14million into his account. He did not expect the stir that his actions would cause, involving bank managers and requests for information. A deposit as large as $14million in cash was not a normal occurrence, and no one was sure of the procedure. But after an hour of rigmarole, John walked out with $1,000 in his wallet, and $13,999,000 in the bank.

It was soon time for dinner, so he sauntered over to the supermarket to buy food and, whilst choosing his favourite chips, heard a familiar voice.

"Did you figure out what that contraption does, John?"

"Hi Alice!" John's face lit up as his mind's eye reverted to seeing them on the bus, and his heart skipped a beat. "I think so. Turns out, it was a time machine."

Alice let out an impulsive laugh that John found so endearing he slid up beside her as his hand touched her hand. "Alice, I..."

"Hey John! How are you, neighbour?" John knew the voice, but it didn't match that of any neighbour. It matched someone he'd become reacquainted with in 1986. He turned, his face reflecting utter disbelief at laying eyes on a much older, full bearded Tom.

John's mouth was open, but no sound came out. Motionless, he stared at this boy-become-man. Tom extended a hand. "Come on! Don't leave me hangin'."

John snapped out of his gormless state, but instead of shaking hands, wrapped his arms around Tom. John's big bear hug turned Tom's face into various contorted expressions, especially when he snuggled in a little too close for comfort.

"OK, that's enough." Tom wriggled out of the embrace.

Alice burst into laughter at Tom's wide-eyed paralysis. Once the blood flow returned to his arms, Tom turned to Alice. "I got that wine, darling. You know that same one we had for our anniversary last month?"

John struggled to hide his shock and disappointment while he watched with envy as Alice gave Tom a cutesy little kiss on his lips.

"You've changed!" John blurted out, trying to do anything other than wallow in the misery of an opportunity missed.

Alice was now confused. "Changed what? His clothes? His underwear? I hope so, for once. You did change them this week, didn't you, Tom? You promised!"

"Oh! Don't mind me, Alice. I'm just some crazed time traveller." At which point he looked at Tom, hoping he might catch onto the implication behind his words.

"Oh. Ohh! Ohhh! Riiiggghhht!" Tom's eyes threatened to pop out of his head, before winking back at John. Seconds later, John and Tom entered their own little Twilight Zone, and Alice stood staring at them with a 'what the hell is wrong with you?' look.

"Why not come round for dinner, neighbour?" Tom's enthusiasm for buddy-buddy time, and John's need to kill time, suited both men.

As soon as they entered the house, Tom pulled John aside. "Darling, I'm going to have a private word with John." They went beyond Alice's earshot, and Tom grabbed John by the shoulders. "You returned today, didn't you?"

"Of course! I'm back the same day I left."

"I knew it! I just knew it!" Tom's glee and huge grin were infectious. "Do you realise I have waited forty years for this day?"

"Listen. The whole you and Alice thing is a lot for me to take in. Now you tell me you've been waiting forty years for me. This all sounds a bit nuts."

"John, all these years, the you I've known has not been, well, you. You know, the you that materialised in a lake, tripped over a dead body, and escaped out of his mom's and dad's upstairs window. At last, I can talk with you about everything that happened all those years ago. And I've been dying to know one thing."

John was sure Tom would have seen the full Back To The Future trilogy by now. "No, my friend, I didn't call myself Clint Eastwood and get hit on by my mom."

"Ha! True? It would've been weird if you had. But no, I was more wondering which theory turned out to be true? The many-worlds interpretation of quantum mechanics or Novikov's self-consistency principle. I have studied both over the years and I would love to get a real-world view."

"Both, I guess. I don't understand why, though." John shook his head. "They seem to oppose each other, but both happen at different times. Anyway, enough of that boring stuff. Have you shacked up with Alice?"

"Why? Was I not married to her in your previous incarnation?"

"No. You were not!"

"Why? Were you married to her?"

"No, Tom. I was her neighbour, but nothing like that ever happened." As John walked away, his head dropped. "Never will now, either."

"Well, I think seeing you on the bus with her gave me a kick in the proverbial ass. After you left, I set my sights on Alice, and we became proper childhood sweethearts. We've had our issues, but we have been together ever since."

"I'm happy for you, dude. And I'm pleased we are still friends. Previously, I never saw you again after 1986. So, this is a welcome surprise."

"Well, you are the same guy I knew forty years ago. But for you it must be a few hours, right? You said you were going to make a detour, though. What did you mean by that?"

John laughed. "That was such a waste of time and effort."

"How do you mean?"

"Remember how I told you about Maradona in the 1986 Football World Cup?"

Tom grabbed John by the hand and started to shake it. "I remember thinking how you had told me about that when it was big news back then."

"Well, I visited Mexico after leaving you, intending to do what I'd said." John retrieved his hand from Tom's clutch. "The aim was to shake his hand so hard, it would prevent him punching the ball.

I managed to meet him for a brief moment in the tunnel before the game, and even shook his hand real hard; you know, like I said I would."

"But he still put the ball in the net with his hand, didn't he?" Tom laughed and shook his head.

"I know. Because I forgot that he's left-handed!" John's eyes rolled backwards as he burst into laughter.

Tom laughed even louder as he grabbed John's hand and shook it again. "You idiot!"

Alice called out for the two of them to come for dinner. "You rang?" John said, as he appeared from the lounge.

"Yeah, I did. You two Lazy-Boys make yourselves useful and set the table."

John thought this would be a great opportunity to prank Alice and lay on the table, whilst Tom placed the cloth over him and set out the plates and condiments on and around him.

"Grow up!" Alice seemed unamused, but still served spaghetti onto a plate that lay on John's belly.

The three of them enjoyed a simple meal together, as John's renewed friendship took on a feeling of surrealism, which was becoming familiar. "I didn't realise until today how much I need both of you in my life." His eyes met Alice's before he turned to meet Tom's. "But now I know I should have told you that years ago."

By the time they had finished eating, it was getting late and Alice asked John if he was ready to head home, but he seemed hesitant. Both John and Tom glanced next door every few minutes, but neither had the inclination for John to leave.

A little after 9.30pm, a flash of light came from the house. John stood and bid them both good night, at which, with a knowing grin, Tom acknowledged it was time his friend went home.

"No, wait." John said to Tom. "I revisited three times after the original trip. We need to see three more flashes."

At 11pm the last flash occurred. The time had come to receive what he had looked forward to the most; a warm doggy welcome from a canine friend, his labrador, Flap. His entrance through the front door brought an excited Flap running, his ears flapping around. Once he saw it was John, who he'd only seen in the living room two minutes earlier, he returned to his bed. The underwhelming welcome disappointed John, who shrugged his shoulders and followed Flap's lead, taking himself to bed.

Next morning the sun stretched its golden fingers across the room. John luxuriated in the embrace of his own bed. Morning had brought a sense of deserved rest, a rarity in recent days.

His mind turned to Joyce and Joe. He wanted to see whether he could find anything about either of them online. It was a long shot, but he'd try it.

With a bit of smart Googling, he came across the Liverpool Museums website which had a whole slew of history and photos all about life in Liverpool during World War Two. Click after click, from one to the next, images of not-so-distant memories fascinated him, until he came across one that stopped him dead. There was Joe. He was looking back at the camera in one of the black and white pictures. John laughed at seeing this young lad once more. He looked some more, and then his mind exploded. There, beside Joe, was Joyce. She was holding onto a man's arm. It was John himself.

"I don't believe it!" he screamed. "I even remember that exact moment. We were wandering down The Strand, and she grabbed hold of my arm. Oh, I'll cherish that forever." His eyes welled up before a tear trickled down his cheek, followed by a fair few more.

He sat and stared at the photo, soaking up pleasures brought by the memories. "Sometimes a memory lasts beyond a lifetime." he thought, as streams of tears now flowed.

It wasn't until he had been studying the picture for about three minutes he noticed there was a man walking towards him and Joyce. John could see his face between his and Joyce's in the picture, and he recognised it. This was the same man that had fought him and Tom outside the cinema. This was unbelievable! The realisation hit him. They must have travelled through the same time corridors between the 1940s and 1980s.

With the image etched into his brain, he relaxed in bed awaiting the day's sole excursion, the monthly Culinary Club. When his stomach's gentle growl reminded him of the hour, he ambled into the kitchen and satisfied its craving with a simple lunch. The clock's steady tick nudged him forward, and he set off for the event, eager to take part.

As he entered the hall, the front row was his only option. Content with the vantage point, he settled in, ready to glean the secrets of the Japanese culinary tradition. The stage, a meticulously arranged table, lay before him. Every tool, each ingredient, had its ordained place.

In the midst of everything, John found his attention drawn to a particular knife. Its familiarity clawed at the edges of his memory. The handle bore a striking blend of yellow and green, the wood a canvas for intricate burls reminiscent of a phoenix's wings. The recognition hit him with the force of a sledgehammer: this was the exact knife that claimed Joyce's life. But how did it stand here, unburdened by the weight of its horrific past, existing in the year 2023?

Aware that answers might be elusive, John pushed his curiosity aside, engrossing himself in the demonstration. The Japanese chef's skill unfolded with an artistry that engaged his creative juices and had John asking so many questions. The chef paid special attention to the knife John had noticed. He even introduced it as a Yuzu Gyuto 210.

The ease with which it sliced through meat and fish, alongside such elegance and precision, warranted the audience's fascination.

As he stood up from his chair, the man sitting beside him surged to the front with a brash arrogance that took John by surprise. In a twist worthy of a magician's sleight of hand, the man's fingers pilfered the knife, sliding it up his sleeve and with a quick swivel, he left. Recognition seeped through the fog of disbelief, and John's realisation crashed upon him like an unexpected storm surge. This was the very embodiment of menace who he had seen in the photo that morning. John's mind raced, the cogs of fate clicking into place. To follow him seemed both an instinctive call and the likelihood of another inevitable beating. Yet follow him, he did.

Whilst in pursuit, his mind swirled with questions about how this man's past appeared to be woven into the tapestry of events that were also historical for John. Could this be a paradoxical dance? It was as if time itself was shifting underfoot, weaving its intricate threads through their entwined narrative.

Conviction bore down on John's conscience, creating a heavy anvil of purpose. He could not let this malevolent player travel through time, knowing the havoc he could sow.

Turning into an alleyway, now close behind, a yawning chasm of uncertainty beckoned. John had stepped into both a metaphorical and physical world of shadows and dead ends. The path was familiar, etched in his memory like an old scar. This was the same alley he had glimpsed Joe and this sinister figure vanish from in 1986.

The man stopped and turned to confront his pursuer. "Who are you? Why are you following me?"

"Why did you take that knife?" John insisted.

"What's it to you?" Hearing John's voice tremble, he swiped the knife from side to side before lunging it towards him.

But John was ready for him and stepped aside like a matador to a charging bull. "I won't let you dabble with time travel. I'm well aware of your identity and your intentions, even if you're not." Conviction and determination now resonated in John's voice.

The knife-wielder's anger boiled over. "You're clueless!" With a violent swipe, he aimed the blade at John's throat. Once again, John dodged a lethal strike. Their tussle erupted into intense close combat, grappling, and twisting as both lives hung in the balance.

John realised, however, this wasn't a favourable situation. Moments later, this hulking figure pinned him to the ground. Desperate to thwart the imminent plunge of the knife into his throat, John summoned up every ounce of strength to push against the downward force being exerted. It seemed futile, like he was fighting a grim dance on the precipice of death itself.

Out of nowhere, a resounding thud echoed through the alleyway, resonating with the impact. The towering antagonist swayed; his focus diverted, as crimson liquid seeped from a vicious gash on his temple. In defiance, he turned to face his attacker, before a second more powerful blow hit him square on the bridge of the nose. His head flung backwards, his face fell forwards, before his body slumped onto the concrete kerb beside John, who lay sprawled on his back, exhausted and gasping for air.

The handsome figure of a man appeared, standing over John clutching a heavy metal pipe. It was Tom.

John caught his breath, relief etched all over his face. "Where did you appear from? You have no idea how glad I am to see you."

Tom's eyes gleamed with a mix of determination and triumph. "I was a couple of rows behind in the hall and saw you slip out. I recognised that crazed lunatic that beat us both up, even after all these years. So, I ran after you, picking up the biggest object I could find."

Tom knelt down to check the man's pulse. Their former assailant was obviously dead, so he pulled John to his feet and hurried him away. "Let's go! We need to disappear." He steadied his friend and led him towards his car parked nearby. With aching muscles and a pounding heart, John was grateful for the safety of the vehicle.

Slumped in the back seat, the world outside seemed distant and insignificant as the journey became a blur. All he wanted was to reach the sanctuary of home.

LAST CHAPTER

THE COUNCIL

John shut the front door; happy to leave the world behind. He had experienced so much in the past couple of weeks. His body battered and mind exhausted, all he wanted was to zone out and watch TV.

With the two time machine devices sitting on a cupboard, his feet up and Bluetooth headphones on, he relaxed in front of anything non-sci-fi or mysterious. Cheers fit the bill, and the laughs took him to a completely different time and place.

During a Cliff Clavin monologue, Flap barked and became excited, so John lifted the headphones. Someone was knocking at the front door. He stayed silent, hoping they'd leave, but they didn't.

The beauty of his uninvited visitor intrigued John. "Hi! Can I help you with something?" He tried to be pleasant, but in his moodiness, the words tumbled from his lips unexpectedly.

"John, can I come in?" This femme fatale seemed to know him already. Her relaxed manner, mixed with a strong intent to chat, was confusing. Despite the instant attraction, John resisted, preferring to be alone. "Are you a Jehovah's Witness? Not into that stuff if you are."

"No John, I'm not here to sell you anything, nor to convert you.

What I have to say will interest you, though." She took a step forward and paused.

"Come on in." He beckoned her inside, giving her little room to get by. "This had better be worth it," he said, as she slid by, her scent lighting up his senses. He decided it was already worth it. She was wearing Marie's perfume.

"My name is Lora. I received a request to meet with you. We've been watching you and are impressed."

"Oh, really? That's a bit freaky." John's face contorted like a five-year-old. "Impressed by what?"

Lora leaned forward. "You're not the first person to travel through time, John. Time travel isn't some random hobby either. It's monitored. It's influenced. And it's a serious business."

Unsure how seriously to take her, John sat with a silly grin on his face. "You mean like Doctor Who and Timelords?" John had always enjoyed the British sci-fi series. That he could be involved with Timelords illuminated his imagination. "Are you from Gallifrey?"

"Who? Sorry, never heard of him."

"Well, who is this 'we' you mentioned?"

Lora laid back in her chair and raised her eyebrows. "The Council monitors the streams of time. Time flows in one direction, like any other stream. The Council looks for disruptions in the normal flow of time. When someone or something travels against the flow, or forwards at an accelerated pace, they see the disturbance."

"How can there be more than one stream of time?" John had been listening closely. "Isn't there only one stream?"

"Any anomaly can form a new timeline, and each timeline is another stream. To be honest with you, John, how you got your hands on the time machines was an anomaly. In fact, it's one we haven't been able to rationalise yet. Anomalies can come thick and fast, and usually, before things get out of hand, The Council steps in. Where necessary, they activate Messengers to influence the streams."

Without some sort of deep analytical explanation of how they could do this, or evidence that they did, John was sceptical. So Lora illustrated her point.

"Who do you think quashed Paula's story? It wasn't any of the obvious candidates. One of our Messengers ascertained details about the editor's private life. That was all they needed to encourage him to pull the story."

"And I thought that was Jane Harding." John was keen to learn more. "So, who are these Messengers?"

"We do the work of The Council to influence outcomes and maintain the status quo. A Messenger doesn't know the why, only what needs to be achieved. Let me make something clear," Lora continued, "Time travel is very common; almost like riding your bike to work. It's important to recognise what it looks like." She explained that despite The Council's power, it was not all powerful. They have successes and make a difference, which is enough to satisfy even more powerful people to retain their services.

"So, who decides what to aid and what to restrict?" John asked.

"The Council. That is their self-appointed role, and they have been overseeing time for… well, for a long time. I'm not sure how else to describe it."

Lora explained some decisions had influenced his journey. Whilst hinting at how his travels intertwined with those of Steve and Joe, she provided no context for him to understand the impacts each traveller had on the others. She did, however, tell him that The Council intervened to prevent Joe from saving his mother.

"What?" John grabbed Lora by the shoulders. "Why would they intervene to stop a son from saving his mother? That makes no sense!"

"It wasn't to be." Lora could give no reason for the decision. "I'm sorry, John, but Joyce cannot survive."

John flung his hands in the air. "So, there is no Novikov or Many World Interpretation in the real world. There is just The Council!"

"There are," Lora began, "but The Council can manipulate things. Unchecked, The Universe would go haywire."

"Oh yeah! That's fair!" John flailed his arms as he resisted the urge to throw Lora out of his house.

"It's a damn sight better than having ten of the same person running around, or having someone give birth to the next Hitler or Jeffrey Dahmer. Don't you think?" Now Lora had her turn at becoming animated.

"I don't know. Time will tell." John walked to the fridge to get a beer. "It shouldn't be for me, you or The Council to decide."

"Not really. It's not time that tells. It's the impact we have in this world that tells the ultimate truth."

"Something still confuses me." John swigged his beer. "How did Tom hear me at the scene of the murder before I was even there?"

Lora's tone changed. "What do you mean?"

"Tom heard me bring a cupboard of glass ornaments crashing to the ground. But that happened before I went to observe the murder."

"You had already been there, John. When you sent yourself to observe the murder, that could not have been your first time there."

"Why didn't I see myself then?"

Lora paused. "Oh, dear! Something's not right. There are rumours of this happening one time before, but that involved a temporal tear overlapping with another universe. As far as I'm aware, this is a fable, but the fabric of time may not be linear, nor without a few tears and rifts here and there. And tears create inexplicable paradoxes."

John stepped back with his beer in hand, but Lora grabbed him by the shoulders. "This explains why The Council sent me to ask you to become a Messenger. They must believe that your impact could have great significance."

The words overwhelmed John, and he was not in the mood to answer. Instead, he saw her to the door. "I'll consider the idea. Come and see me in six months. I might have something for you then."

Lora turned, walked back up the steps, put her foot in the door's jamb, and said, "After what you told me, there may not be any six months if you say no." Without further resistance, she left.

Her sincerity and the ominous tone in her voice flustered John.

He returned to Cheers. The idea of making a life-changing decision could wait. It was time to chillax for the rest of the evening.

The next day dawned with John refreshed and ready to take on the world once again. He walked into town, unsure why something wasn't quite right. Soon enough, he bumped into someone that would show his world had changed, or was about to.

"I am so sorry," the diminutive man, wearing shades and a hoody, said as he nearly knocked John to the ground.

"I could have banged my head on the sidewalk. You need to be careful, man!" John waited for a response, but only an awkward pause ensued. That was until both men made a popping sound with their lips.

"Who are you?" John's nostrils flared and without hesitation he unhooded this familiar stranger.

The man removed his shades. "Hi, dude."

There, before John, stood … John. A little older, tanned and with even less hair, but gelled with such style that the younger guy made a mental note for when he got home.

John's thoughts ran away with him. "Woah! He smells so good! If this is me in a few years, I love how much cooler I'll become." And he found it hard not to stare or come in closer for a deeper whiff.

"Yes, I do, and thank you." The elder John said with a smile, as the younger glimpsed a sparkle reflecting off the gleaming whiteness of his teeth. John's own voice emanated from this slick dude, peering over the top of his shades.

"Are you for real? You're reading my mind. Do you have ESP?"

"No, but I do have a great memory. Right now, though, listen to me. You need to join the fight for what's right. We could benefit from you becoming me."

"Hang on! Hang on! Slow down. I am meeting myself from a different time. The time-space continuum should be collapsing, as we are creating a paradox that should collapse time in on its..."

"Stop with the dumbass theorising." The older guy gave him a slap across the face. "I don't understand all the rules or laws or whatever it's called about temporal mobility, and I've been riding this rollercoaster for a while now. But I do know that I could slap you around; time and space wouldn't give a crap."

"OK, but how are you telling me this? I have not even decided to join your cause so that I can return to now and give myself this message. This is impossible! Why are you coming back to convince me? I must have already decided without you telling me."

John the elder sidled up with a smirk on his face and said, "Lora convinced me initially, but you might say I got my priorities a bit confused with her, so we decided I should do the convincing myself. This way, there is no chance of any funny business."

Young John backed off. "You got that right, bucko! Even if you have sexed me up." He leaned in to take another whiff. "You do smell fan-ta-stic."

"Relax. Your time will come." Maturity resonated from the wrinkly John. "We need you, man. It's only once you travel down this path that you'll see how convoluted it gets. But there is no other way."

After making his pitch, the elder John hoped to protect his protégé. "Oh, your fingerprints are a hot item, by the way. Try to avoid any run-ins with the law. Believe me, it won't go well."

John considered everything about his recent travels as the two returned to his/their home, and Joyce and Joe came to mind. He found that photo again on liverpoolmuseums.org.uk and reminisced, showing it to his other self.

"You sound so sad. Why is that?" the older guy asked.

"You know why. Joyce was murdered."

"Is that so?"

"Stop it! This is no joke!" Like his earlier walk, something was different, bringing back an inexplicable unease. "The man in the picture between me and…" He stopped and stared at the photo. The man between him and Joyce. Where was the face he had seen before? The man was not there.

His heart raced and his thoughts ran a marathon in a minute. "Hang on. I need to know something."

For the next couple of hours, the older John sat back and watched as junior used all his expertise at finding people online; signing up for ancestry.co.uk and searching every births and deaths website in Britain.

After much angst and a fair few coffees, the investigation came to fruition. In black and white, right before their eyes:

Joyce Tuttle: Born Liverpool 17 April 1916 Died Liverpool 21 October 1986

"Woah! She lived! Lora was wrong." John's whole body felt like it was floating. A weight of sadness fell from his soul. He turned to his older, friendly self and said, "Lora doesn't know everything."

The sexy senior turned to his younger, friendly self. "No, she doesn't. But she was on the right track. Welcome to the Multiverse, my friend." Without another word, he sauntered over to the time machines and held them in his hands. "You know what's special about these?" he asked, turning to look over his shoulder.

"Certainly do!" John watched a scowl form on his friend's face.

The scowl melted away as a smile replaced it. "Nothing." He raised his hand that held the strange-looking contraption, as he had done many times before and threw it onto the hard tiled floor. In an instant, mechanical innards shot out in all directions.

"No!" screamed his companion.

The other hand holding the watch rose in a similar movement, and John leapt at his older self. However, it was in vain. He landed on him and the two collapsed into a heap of Johns on the floor, the watch was already a mess of broken parts in amongst the other broken fragments.

"What the hell are you doing?" The more youthful man grabbed a startled older version of himself by the scruff of the neck and shook him vigorously. "I want to use that again, you crazy, sad, lonely loser! That was to be my escape from this demoralising existence. What am I meant to do now?" His grip loosened as he slumped to the ground, his head now buried in his arms.

Composed once more and rising to his feet, John senior slapped his counterpart on the back. "Get over yourself. Where we're going, those devices will not suffice. Now, strap yourself in for an adventure beyond any this universe can offer."

The End … for now!